Bargaining for
the Billionaire

ALSO BY JM STEWART

Bidding on the Billionaire
Winning the Billionaire

Bargaining for the Billionaire

JM STEWART

FOREVER
YOURS

New York   Boston

Copyright © 2016 by JM Stewart
Excerpt from *Claiming the Billionaire* © 2016 by JM Stewart
Cover design by Elizabeth Turner
Cover image © Colin Anderson/GettyImages
Cover copyright © 2016 by Hachette Book Group, Inc.

Forever Yours
Hachette Book Group
1290 Avenue of the Americas
New York, NY 10104
forever-romance.com
twitter.com/foreverromance

First Edition: September 2016
Forever Yours is an imprint of Grand Central Publishing.
The Forever Yours name and logo are trademarks of Hachette Book Group, Inc.

The publisher is not responsible for websites (or their content) that are not owned by the publisher.

The Hachette Speakers Bureau provides a wide range of authors for speaking events. To find out more, go to www.hachettespeakersbureau.com or call (866) 376-6591.

ISBN 978-1-4555-9224-1 (ebook edition)
ISBN 978-1-4555-9225-8 (print on demand edition)

For my readers.
Thanks for taking a chance on me.

Bargaining for the Billionaire

Chapter One

Dread sank in Madison O'Riley's stomach as the musical jingle of her phone announced the arrival of a message. Any other day, that sound could bring a smile. It would've meant she'd gotten a text from one of her two best friends: usually Christina confirming details for a girls' night out or Hannah sending a picture of her three-month-old daughter, Emily.

Tonight, however, that sound meant the message she'd been waiting for had arrived. For a moment, she could only stare at the sender's name, blinking on the small, black screen. Was she really ready for this?

"Is that him?" Seated on the couch across from her, Hannah leaned forward, bracing her elbows on her knees.

Maddie lifted her gaze, peering across the coffee table. Seated on the couch, Hannah grinned, ear to flippin' ear, her dark brows all the way up into her hairline. The rat. Christina, at least, tried to hide her excited smile. More refined, she sat with her long legs crossed and her hands folded in her lap. She looked calm and unperturbed, but the glimmer in her eyes gave her away. Both women clearly waited for the "deets."

Maddie sighed and shook her head. "How did I let you two rope me into this?"

Okay, so she knew the answer. Both of the other women had found their soul mates. They were all so damned happy it made her flat-out jealous. At this point, she was stalling. This blind date they'd "encouraged" her into should be a good thing. She hadn't dated in three years, and they were right. It was time. This hare-brained scheme provided a middle ground. After all, what harm could a little flirting do?

Hannah straightened, leaning back into the sofa cushions. "Because you're lonely, babe. You said it yourself. But you also said you weren't ready for another relationship." She shrugged. "It worked for me. I got to know Cade online. Start there. It's just Gchat. If you decide you don't like him, you don't have to go through with the auction."

Christina flashed one of her smiles, the soft kind that always managed to melt the nerves raging in Maddie's stomach. There was something so calming about Christina.

"Hannah's right. There will be hundreds of women willing to take him off your hands. But he's nice. I promise. And he's not a *toad*, as you so aptly put it. I gather only the best for my auctions." Christina grinned, giving her a sassy little wink that had Maddie hard-pressed not to laugh.

Her two best friends couldn't have been more different. Where Hannah was quiet and shy and often uncertain of herself, Christina was all elegance but bold as brass. Maddie had known Hannah since her days spent working in the marketing department of Bradbury Books, a mid-sized publisher on the rise. Long before they'd taken a walk on the wild side and opened their little bookstore four years ago.

She'd met Christina through Hannah. Christina was Hannah's husband's twin sister. They'd officially become friends when Christina had asked for help planning Hannah's bachelorette party. She'd made an instant lifelong friend that night.

Hannah had had an online affair, one that eventually led to her falling in love and getting married. Hannah had taken a chance and met Cade in person. What began as a two-week fling while he was in Seattle had become more.

Exactly how Maddie now found herself staring at a Gchat from a stranger, nausea swirling in her stomach. She wouldn't exactly call herself celibate. After her breakup with Grayson three years ago, she'd sworn off men and dating. Which meant it wasn't raining men in her world, either. It didn't help that she'd trust another man when little pink elephants flew south for the winter.

Hannah reached out a socked foot and nudged her toe. "Oh, go on. Answer him. What harm can it do? He doesn't have your number, just your e-mail address, and believe me, nobody in the world is going to know who Mad Hatter Three Thousand is."

Maddie's mouth went dry, a dull pounding starting in her temples. "Oh, God, I think I'm going to be sick."

Her hand trembled as she picked up her cell from the coffee table. She swiped her finger up the screen, then tapped the Gchat icon. The message that popped up was innocuous, really, but her phone shook in her palm anyway.

BookNerd: Hey. Christina gave me your e-mail address. Apparently, you're my date for the auction this year. ;)

Christina came from a wealthy family. Founder and head of a local charity her family made a sizable donation to every year, her "baby" was a bachelor auction, carried out in the name of raising money for breast cancer research. Maddie had met her at the auction, where Cade had been one of the bachelors.

As with every year, twelve hunky guys were being auctioned off for a good cause. Any other time, she'd have been all over that. She had no desire to date, or God forbid, fall in love again, but she was a woman, after all. With needs and yearnings, and she missed things like sex. She had a sore need to get laid. She wanted the weight of a man's body pressing her into the mattress, yearned for a real cock pounding into her, hot and hard and not made of rubber. She wanted the huff of his warm breath on her neck, and by God, she ached for the luscious rush of an orgasm she didn't have to give to herself.

She'd grown damn tired of her Battery Operated Boyfriend, otherwise lovingly referred as to as B.O.B, but sex with a real man meant complications, which she flat out didn't do. Flirting with a hot guy made her nerves shake, but could make her whole night. Knowing the men Christina chose for her auctions were all successful, with muscles on top of muscles, didn't hurt, either. Christina had excellent taste.

This year, Maddie had a date with someone she'd never met and wouldn't meet until the night of the auction. Exactly two weeks from today.

She glanced down at her phone again. His e-mail address seemed harmless enough. It hinted that they had something in common—books. Her stomach still wobbled all the same, and she cursed her nerves. It wasn't like her to be so nervous. She was a people person, damn it. Besides, she couldn't stay single forever. If she truly wanted a night of hot, sweaty sex, she had to get back up on that horse. And it started with this Gchat.

Her thumbs hovered over the on-screen keyboard. "What on earth do I say to him?"

Christina gave a soft, airy laugh. "You could start with hello."

"Hello." Maddie nodded. "Right. I can do that."

Oh, God help me, here goes nothing. Her fingers shook so hard she had to type the word twice.

MadHatter3000: Hi

She swallowed past the lump of fear stuck in her throat, punched SEND and waited. His reply popped up almost immediately, sending the butterflies in her stomach into an uproar.

BookNerd: How are you?

Maddie grinned. Okay, this was easy. This she could do. She punched in another quick reply.

MadHatter3000: Good, thx. U?

BookNerd: Oh, I'm fairly certain my night just got a whole lot better.

Maddie rolled her eyes. Oh, that was cheesy.

MadHatter3000: Ur a flirt, aren't u?

Once again, his reply was instantaneous.

BookNerd: Guilty as charged.

Across from her, Christina arched a brow in silent question.

Hannah sat forward again, bouncing on the couch like an excited child. "What'd he say?"

Maddie pursed her lips and lifted her gaze. "He's flirting with me."

Hannah's grin nearly split her face in half. "That's not a bad thing, Madds."

Maddie shrugged. The knots in her stomach weren't so convinced. "I suppose."

Christina smiled over the top of her wineglass, her eyes gleaming with playful impishness. "This is where you flirt back. If you want some company after the auction, you're going to have to leave a trail of breadcrumbs for the man."

Maddie laughed and shook her head. Christina was right, of course. If she wanted an orgasm from somebody other than B.O.B., she'd have to come out of her shell a bit. After all, wasn't that what she'd told Hannah to do? When Hannah had been in the same place two years ago, trying to decide if a fling with Cade was what she wanted, Maddie had urged her to live in the moment or else she'd regret it. And Maddie had a lot of regrets. What would that weekend with Grayson have amounted to had she not gotten cold feet?

She sighed. "Okay, okay. Let me think. I'm rusty at this."

She tapped her finger on the side of her phone, thinking.

The words popped into her thoughts seconds later, and Maddie typed and hit send before she lost the nerve to say them.

MadHatter3000: Confident aren't we? Don't think a date means ur automatically getting into my pants. ;)

She stuffed the nail of her index finger into her mouth and waited. Had she been too rude? Too presumptuous?

Seconds ticked by before his reply came back. Just long enough for the doubts to close around her throat. She had to be insane for agreeing to this.

BookNerd: Are you challenging me?

Her head filled with visions of what he must look like. Tall, dark and handsome, like Cade and Sebastian. Full of muscles for sure. And sitting somewhere doing exactly what she was—his phone in his hand, waiting on her replies. The thought had her heart hammering a giddy beat, and her palms sweating, but damn. This could be addicting. It was the most fun she'd had since…well, since Grayson.

Thoughts of her ex had the beginnings of panic clawing their way up her throat. Hands shaking in earnest now, Maddie leaned forward and set her phone down on the coffee table. "I can't do this. This isn't me."

Hannah set down her glass of soda and pushed off the couch, coming to perch on the arm of Maddie's recliner. She looped an arm around Maddie's shoulders, hugging her tightly. "Yes, you can. You're the first person in the store to pounce on any halfway decent-looking man who walks through the door. You're an incorrigible flirt. Why does this one make you so nervous? It's just a date."

Maddie shook her head, memories rising over her. "When I flirt with the guys in the store it's just fun. I haven't had an actual date in three years."

Grayson Lockwood wasn't the first guy she'd fallen in love with, but that breakup had hit the hardest. Discovering his lies had destroyed everything she'd sworn they had and made her feel like a hopeless fool. She'd discovered on the front page of a local newspaper that he wasn't just another editor working his way up through the rungs of the publishing company they'd worked for at the time. He *owned* the company, had inherited it from his father when he died.

Which meant he'd lied to her the whole time she'd known him. His lies had made her question their entire relationship. Was anything he told her real? Or was she just part of the charade? Did she really know him at all?

Like Matt, in college. She'd met Matt originally in Biology class. He'd chatted her up, playing the nice guy, the geek, helping her with her homework. Then one night, he'd invited her to a frat party on campus. He'd fed her spiked drinks, and she'd woken up the next morning alone, confused and violated.

Grayson wasn't Matt, but he'd still lied to her about who he was. Liars. She despised them. A deep pain crushed her chest every time she thought about it, because it brought her screeching back to that awful night in college. Learning the truth about Grayson had only reinforced what she already knew: that men couldn't be trusted. Because they all lied.

In the end she'd decided she didn't want to know which parts of their relationship were truth and which were more lies. She couldn't do it. She couldn't put her trust in another man who'd only hurt her again.

Her phone pinged again from the coffee table. She and Hannah both turned. Another reply flashed on the black screen.

BookNerd: Nervous?

"Do what you do best, Madds. He's just a guy, and you need this. You want this. You said so yourself." Hannah squeezed her tight then released her and resumed her seat on the sofa. "Try being honest with him. Always worked for me and Cade."

Maddie sighed. She had to admit, Hannah had a point. Cade was good for Hannah. He'd opened her up and given her confidence. Hannah no longer hid the scars that cut across her face. The two of them were so damned happy Maddie couldn't even envy them. Hannah deserved to be happy. More to the point, if honesty worked for them, maybe it would work for her, too.

She picked up her phone, typing in a more honest reply.

MadHatter3000: I don't usually do this sort of thing.

BookNerd: Honestly? Me either.

This reply soothed the knot in her chest. His confession, however, filled her with questions.

MadHatter3000: So y r u?

BookNerd: Because I told Christina the only way I'd partic-ipate was if she made sure I didn't end up with some 80 y/o woman or her lonely daughter.

Ah, now they were getting somewhere.

MadHatter3000: So, u don't want to do this, either.

Knowing her date didn't feel so certain either wasn't the most promising prospect she'd ever had, but the nausea swirling in her stomach eased by a large degree. At least she wasn't alone in her nervousness.

BookNerd: Not originally. I don't usually participate in these things. I have no desire to end up as someone's plaything. But I have to admit I'm enjoying this. Christina mentioned that you don't trust easily. Truth is, neither do I.

Maddie smiled. Beginning to finally relax, she couldn't resist teasing him.

MadHatter3000: How do u know I'm not an ugly hag?

BookNerd: lol I've known Christina since high school. I trust her judgment.

Hold the phone. Christina had distinctly left out that little detail.

Maddie peered across the coffee table at Christina. "You know him?"

Christina smiled. "Of course. You didn't think I'd set you up with someone I didn't? I've known him since high school. Gr—I mean, Dave is a nice guy."

Maddie narrowed her gaze on Christina. It had almost sounded like Christina was about to say another name. In fact, since this whole thing began, Christina and Hannah had had *secret* written all over them. Their heads were always bent together in a quiet conversation that ceased the minute Maddie joined them. She'd let them convince her it was nothing, but this time, she had to know.

She pursed her lips and pointed a finger. "All right, what is it you're not telling me about him?"

Christina held up her free hand in mock surrender. "Nothing, I promise. You just picked an excellent wine is all. I'm afraid I haven't indulged in a while, and this Moscato is delicious. It's going straight to my head."

Hannah jerked her gaze to Christina and raised her brows. "Why haven't you been indulging? You love wine. You always indulge."

Christina flushed to the roots of her dark hair and glanced down, brushing invisible bits from her lap. "I think seeing you and Cade with little Emily is getting to him, because Sebastian suddenly wants a baby. And I thought I might be pregnant for a while. False alarm."

Hannah squealed and threw her arms around Christina, hugging her tight, much to Christina's dismay. "Oooh, I'm so happy for you. He's going to make a great dad."

Momentarily distracted, Maddie couldn't resist a giggle. This was what had drawn them all together in the first place. They were all so much alike. Teasing came easily, and the laughter flowed freely. Now, it had her mind shifting gears. Christina and Sebastian had been married almost a year now. She'd married her brother's best friend. Having known each other most of their lives and been in love with each other for half that, the two were the poster children for typical newlyweds. They had a penchant for disappearing together. Christina always returned a little flushed. Sebastian usually came back with a swagger and a grin, like he'd conquered the world.

"The point being"—Christina narrowed her gaze, eyeing them one by one—"I've known him for a long time.

He always was a bit of a loner. We're a lot alike in that respect. Growing up, he was a fellow nerd. Smart, worked hard to get good grades. I've been trying to get him to participate in the auction since its inception, but he's always refused. This year I managed to convince him, but only if I promised to fix the game for him. He didn't want to end up with a date he'd regret or someone who'd make his life hell afterward."

Maddie arched a brow. "Isn't that cheating?"

"Yes, but it's for a good cause. The purpose is to raise money and awareness." Hannah shrugged. "Besides, everybody always has fun, and there are eleven other bachelors."

Maddie's phone pinged again, another message flashing on the dark screen. She squeezed her eyes shut, afraid to look. "I still don't know if I can do this. Grayson took a lot out of me."

"You have to get back on that horse sometime, Madds. If you want to find Prince Charming, you have to kiss a few toads." Hannah nudged her with a socked foot again. "Go on. Pick it up and flirt with the man. Have a good time. See where it takes you. It doesn't have to be any more complicated than that. What's it going to hurt?"

Maddie opened her eyes and sighed. They were right. She'd never be able to move on by playing celibate and dead. She leaned forward, snatched her phone off the coffee table, and peered at the message.

BookNerd: Did I scare you off already?

She arched a brow at Christina. "Is he really good looking or was that lip service? Be honest."

Christina winked, mischievous and amused. "Oh, I think he'll make a *mighty* fine horse."

Maddie laughed softly. "You two are terrible, you know that?"

Only between the three of them would they ever say something so audacious, but it was what she loved about Hannah and Christina. They could relax around each other, say things they might not otherwise. It made them excellent friends. She never held back with them. It was also what had made her give in to this date, despite everything inside of her screaming what a bad idea it was. They'd always have her back, no matter what.

Hannah pursed her lips and waved a hand at her. "Oh, come off it. You're thinking it and you know it."

Maddie shook her head. "I am getting awful tired of B.O.B."

Christina and Hannah broke into a fit of giggles. Maddie drew up her inner vixen, beaten and worn out though she was, and typed the first halfway playful thing she could think of.

MadHatter3000: I don't scare so easily. U just better have ur A-game on.

His reply arrived seconds later.

BookNerd: Ohh, sweetheart. Consider that challenge accepted.

Chapter Two

You know, she's going to be pissed when she discovers it's you, that you're not some random bachelor."

Grayson Lockwood grunted in answer but didn't bother looking up from his laptop. He didn't need to see her to face to know Cassie was giving him "the look." Cassandra Stephanopoulos had been his best friend since tenth grade. They'd met in an English class she was failing. Their friendship had begun when she'd asked him to tutor her. More to the point, they'd had this conversation before. He'd gone over the argument at least a million times in his head. This charade would no doubt fail like the one three years ago, but he had to take the chance.

Agreeing to take part in Christina McKenzie's bachelor auction had been a spur of the moment decision. Every year she tried to rope him into participating, and every year he refused. He had no desire to be paraded around like livestock, waiting to go on a date with a woman who'd no doubt try to wrangle herself into his life and his pockets.

Except Christina had shown up this time with backup, in the form of Hannah Miller, now apparently Hannah McKenzie. He'd taken one look at Hannah and the wheels had started spinning. He'd worked alongside Hannah at Bradbury Books for over a year and a half, while on his little mission to recoup his adoptive father's good name. He knew darn well she and Maddie O'Riley were joined at the hip, and that they now owned a small, eclectic bookshop downtown. In her sweet smile as Christina attempted to persuade him into participating, the opportunity of a lifetime had presented itself.

He hit SEND on Gchat and lifted his gaze. Cassie stood before him with one hand planted on her hip and one dark brow arched in silent challenge. Short and petite she might be. Never mind that her pixie haircut made her appear as if she were still in college, despite that she was twenty-eight. But when she wanted to be, Cassie could be damn fierce.

He released a heavy breath, relenting to her inquisition. "I know. I'll admit it. I may very well have lost my mind by thinking this up, but I've been waiting three years for the chance to finally explain myself to her. I can't let this opportunity pass me by. Not this time."

He'd done everything wrong with Maddie. She shouldn't have had to find out about his charade in the goddamn newspaper. A little over four years ago, rumors had started that he'd gained his position as CEO of Bradbury Books because his father owned the company. There were also those who knew where he'd come from and speculated that he hadn't gained his position through hard work, but because Arthur had merely taken pity on a poor street kid. It implied, of course, that Arthur had been a soft-hearted, but feeble-minded old fool. That he wasn't capable of running his own company, and by default, that Grayson was unfit to take his place after his death.

Arthur Bradbury had been the only man in his life to prove himself worthy of being called *father*. He'd been a strict, but kind old man, one who'd taken a dirty kid off the streets and given him a home. He deserved better than to be remembered that way, and Grayson vowed to prove them wrong.

So, he'd set out to earn the trust of the employees and board members. He wanted to prove he'd earned his position by working his tail off and the only way he could think to do that was to show them, by working down in the trenches with them. He'd started where everyone else did—entry level, with the intention of working his way up. Eventually, he'd reveal himself and set his new plans for the company into motion.

Except his plan backfired. Six months into the charade, someone discovered the truth and leaked the story to a local newspaper for a buck. Maddie discovered he'd lied to her about who he was before he had the chance to tell her. She'd read that newspaper article and assumed the worst, then ended their relationship point blank. In his defense, he hadn't known at first whether or not he could trust her. And then fear had gotten to him.

His childhood before he met Arthur wasn't a story he liked to remember and it wasn't something he shared easily. Other than Cassie, not many knew the ugly world Arthur had pulled him from. Most people assumed he'd been a runaway. He'd worried about Maddie's reaction. Would his past matter to her? When he eventually showed her his back, would the scars disgust her?

He should've told her long before that damn article ever printed. For three years he'd lamented his decision. Now he had the chance to fix it. She might very well walk away from him again, but he had to try. The problem was, Maddie wouldn't give him the time of day.

"I let fear get in the way last time, Cassie. I can't do it again."

Cassie shook her head, empathy rising in her eyes. She'd been his best friend for fifteen years; she knew the life he'd lived before Arthur found him. She knew as well the shame that life had stained on his soul. He'd worked hard to move beyond the street urchin he'd once been, eating out of the garbage and begging for money in order to make it through the day. He'd worked damn hard, too, to make sure Arthur never regretted bringing him home that night.

"I've said it before, Gray, and I'll say it again. Anyone who holds your past against you isn't worth it." She smiled and her dark brown eyes filled with a familiar, mischievous glint. "You do realize when she finds out, she isn't just going to be mad. If she's a typical redhead, she's likely to lop your balls off and hang them from the top of the Space Needle."

He grinned. She was right, of course. If you were on her

good side, Maddie could be as sweet as they came. If you were on her bad side…well, Maddie tended to hold a grudge.

He chuckled and transferred his laptop to the couch beside him. "Yes, and I look forward to the challenge."

He let his wounded pride get in the way last time. He'd let her go, and he wouldn't do it again. This time, he had to tell her what she really meant to him, that he loved her. Because he missed her. He regretted not fighting for her when he had the chance. That weekend three years ago, he'd planned a romantic getaway for the two of them, a little cabin on the coast. He'd planned to tell her everything and let the cards fall where they may but had hoped she'd give him the benefit of the doubt.

Then that blasted newspaper article printed, spouting half-truths. They too had suggested that he hadn't earned his position. Had even gone so far as to accuse him of trying to con a kind old man. When he'd threatened to sue for defamation of character, they'd printed a retraction a week later, but the result was still the same. Maddie wouldn't so much as give him the time of day, and he'd been so hurt, he'd convinced himself he didn't need her.

A musical ping sounded from his laptop, signaling an incoming message, and Maddie's Gchat box popped onto his screen. Of course, he knew it was her. While working alongside her three years ago, they'd spent a lot of time e-mailing and chatting. Somewhere buried on his laptop, he had well over a year's worth of e-mails saved. He'd know that username in his sleep.

Cassie frowned and shook her head.

"That's my cue to go. I have a dinner date. I also have no desire to watch you dig your own grave." She crossed the room and bent over him, wrapping an arm around his shoulders and squeezing. "Don't let this drag out. Tell her. Soon."

When she pulled back, he smiled at her. "She'll find out at the auction. That's the whole idea. I want her to get to know *me* again, and that won't happen if she knows it's me. She'll shut me down before I even get a word out. At least this way, I have a fighting chance."

Cassie furrowed her brow as she straightened and shoved a stern finger at him. "Balls, Gray. Mark my words, you're going to lose yours." She leaned over to peck his cheek, then shook her head and made her way to the front door, her heels clicking softly on the hardwood floors. "Dinner. Soon. You owe me."

He set his laptop on his knees again and darted a glance over his shoulder. "Tomorrow night good for you? I'll even let you pick the place."

"Tomorrow is wonderful. I should be home by seven." The door opened with a soft crack and a whoosh of air. "And something expensive."

Grayson chuckled. "I almost feel sorry for the poor bastard you end up with. He's going to need deep pockets."

It was almost an insult, but he knew Cassie wouldn't be offended. It was a playful conversation they'd had before. He preferred simple, cheap food. Old habits died hard. A good burger was a good burger, and he couldn't see spending fifty bucks for one because the establishment called itself "up-scale." Cassie, however, had grown up spoiled. Her father owned a small chain of Greek Restaurants and had doted on her. Cassie, jewelry designer extraordinaire, had developed expensive tastes.

As expected, she laughed, light, airy and amused. "Honey, I've got my own pockets. He just needs to have stamina."

Grayson laughed, and the door closed behind her. Alone now, he returned his attention to his laptop, reading Maddie's message. Christ, he'd missed her. She had passion. Technically, they'd never made love, and if all went according to plan, they wouldn't anytime soon. At least not yet. He had plans to sweep one Madison O'Riley clean off her stubborn heels. He wanted her trust first. Then he planned to make love to her long and slow. But the thought of her at home, flirting with him, was enough to light his fire.

MadHatter3000: is this your idea of an A-game? Flowers are really cliché, you know.

Grayson grinned. Two days had passed since their first chat. He hadn't spoken to her since. Meetings and book releases had kept him busy. Today, he'd decided to take the charade one step forward. He'd sent her flowers. He was leaving breadcrumbs. By the time the auction came, she'd have enough pieces to put together the puzzle. The first one was, of course, his Gchat username. He'd chosen it on purpose. The second? He'd sent her white lilies. The exact kind he'd given her for her birthday when they first started dating three years ago. Mixed in, of course, were some brighter tones so it wasn't too easy for her to guess.

BookNerd: Flowers are classic. If you ask me, they're never cliché or out of style. Are they too much?

Seconds passed in silence. Having to keep himself in check was killing him. He wanted to ask her what she was wearing, what she was doing, what perfume she'd put on this morning. None of which he could, because she had no idea who he was. He was essentially a stranger to her. It drove him nuts, and yet lured him at the same time. He couldn't wait to get to know her again, to open her up. Hell, simply being able to talk to her at all made him want to beat his chest.

A full minute passed before her reply popped up.

MadHatter3000: No. They're beautiful. Thanks. I'm not sure what to say, though. I didn't expect it. How'd you know where to send them?

BookNerd: I asked Christina to send.

That, at least, was true, though mostly because Maddie could check if she chose to.

Her instantaneous reply filled his mind with visions of her. Seated on that God awful purple couch in her living room. She was on her laptop for sure, because she spelled out her words. Maddie tended to revert to what everyone else did when texting. He loathed text shorthand. It also didn't look good coming from the CEO of a publishing company.

MadHatter3000: That explains how you knew my favorite flower.

BookNerd: I asked her to send you something beautiful. But you probably get flowers all the time.

MadHatter3000: LOL. That would require me having a man. Which I don't.

That made him grin in spite of himself. The thought of her making love to another man made him want to dent something and filled him with a crushing regret. The first year after their break up, he'd lamented that the most—that she wasn't his anymore.

He might not have a chance in hell of winning Maddie back, but this, at least, gave him hope. That she'd even agreed to this blind date meant she wasn't seeing anyone, now at least. He shouldn't ask, and although curiosity might very well have killed the cat, he had to know.

BookNerd: May I ask why not?

Grayson waited for what seemed forever, and her lack of answer grated on his nerves. Had he pushed her too hard? Damn it all to hell. He hated pretending he didn't know her. There were so many things he yearned to tell her.

Finally, her reply popped onto his screen.

MadHatter3000: What, no comment about this being your lucky break?

Grayson grinned. Unless he was mistaken, she was flirting with him. That was a damn good sign.

He drew a deep breath. *Play it cool, Lockwood.*

BookNerd: Nope. Figured that was a given, everything considered. It's really none of my business, but seeing as we're supposed to be getting to know each other, I figured this was a safe area. Start with the basics.

MadHatter3000: I'm surprised. No sexual comments yet. Impressive. For most men, the basics would've started with measurements. That's how this works, right?

Her words taunted him with all those things he yearned

to ask. Memories past lodged themselves in his mind. All those late night chats, when he should have been working but had become distracted by her. An innocent, *"Hello, hope you're having a good night,"* from her had launched a thousand e-mails between them, each one hotter than the last, and usually ended in him picking up his phone. He'd tell her everything he wanted to do to her, and the conversations always ended in phenomenal orgasms for both of them. They might not have made love, but they'd done a hell of a lot. To this day the little noise she made when she came still haunted his dreams.

His fingers trembled over the keyboard as he struggled with his reply. What he wanted to say versus what he ought to say.

Don't say it, Lockwood. Keep it light. Keep it neutral.

That's what he told himself, at least. His fingers, however, didn't appear to be listening. Curiosity had downright slayed that cat.

BookNerd: Not necessarily. Are you telling me you'd actually share?

The clock on the wall across from him ticked-tick-ticked out the seconds. His gut knotted and his nerves frayed. He was so damn close yet so far away.

Edgy and restless, he deposited his laptop onto the couch beside him and surged to his feet, pacing the living room spread out before him. He stared out the glass that made up the far wall, at the lights dotting the other houses around him. Lake Union spread out before him, calm and serene. The neighborhood was dead silent and memories echoed around him. All those late night conversations filled his head. Three years ago, he'd have told her, *"Describe what you're wearing tonight, baby..."*

For all her bravado, Maddie was a traditional girl. On their first date, she'd told him she didn't sleep around, that before she made love to him, she had to trust him. It had taken him six months to make it past first base, and he'd considered himself damn lucky for that. Which meant he had to cool his jets and follow her lead this time as well.

Behind him, his laptop pinged with the announcement of a new message. He jogged back to the couch, plopping down with all the finesse of an excited eight year old. His laptop bounced on the soft cushions and a quiet laugh escaped him. Hell. Cassie was right. Maddie had him well and thoroughly by the cock.

He set his laptop once again on his knees and read her message.

MadHatter3000: I might. So long as we get one thing clear.

His heart hammered. Damn, he hadn't expected her to say that. He'd expected her to shut him down. Now, he was intrigued.

BookNerd: All right. Lay it on me.

MadHatter3000: I'm not looking for permanent. Just some fun. That's probably TMI, but you asked and I'm an honest kind of girl. When our date at the auction ends, this ends.

Grayson tipped his head back and laughed. It seemed they really were in the same place, neither one really able to move on. It gave him hope, and awakened a certain part of his anatomy he was sure once had shriveled up from lack of use. Christ, he was hopeless. A few words of encouragement and he was hard as steel. His cock strained, pushing uncomfortably against the zipper of his tailored slacks.

BookNerd: Are you telling me you're just looking for sex?

MadHatter3000: And if I am?

For a moment, Grayson could only stare at his screen, dumbfounded. His cock twitched, encouraging him to pick up that particular breadcrumb and run like hell with it. For the first time in a long time, he'd have a fantasy that didn't include old memories, but another living, breathing participant.

Well, I'll be damned.

His fingers shook with a heady mix of adrenaline and arousal as he punched in a reply.

BookNerd: Sweetheart, I'll admit that little tidbit has me harder than a brass rod. No fair teasing with comments like that. ;) But I think we should take this one step at a time.

He meant that. He had no desire to scare her off before they'd even begun. That her reply once again popped up seconds later, however, didn't help the snugness of his pants.

MadHatter3000: Please don't tell me you're a traditional guy.

Grayson dragged a hand through his hair. Christ. At this rate, he'd never get any sleep tonight. He'd hoped to loosen her up. Never in a million years had he expected her to respond. What the hell did he say to her now?

He drew a deep breath and released it as the answer hit him. Honesty. As much as possible given the circumstances of this charade, honesty was always the best policy.

BookNerd: Actually, I am. But I meant that I don't want you to think this was my entire plan, to seduce you. That's not who I am. I'm kind of going with the flow. Though, truth be told, I'm enjoying this.

MadHatter3000: Me, too. So tell me what you look like. Christina was vague on the deets.

Another knot formed in his gut as the answer to her innocent query flitted through his mind. Christina was vague on purpose.

BookNerd: 6'3", brown hair, brown eyes.

That was the truth, at least.

BookNerd: Your turn.

MadHatter3000: Workout?

A soft laugh escaped him. Apparently, she intended to torture him before she told him what she looked like. Oh, he knew, had long since memorized all the lines and angles of her face, all the natural hues in her hair, and the little gold flecks around her pupils. But he was curious as hell what she'd actually tell him. This was a bold side of Maddie he'd never seen before. It both intrigued and saddened him. What had she been through in the last three years that she'd decided to jump in feet first?

During an intimate conversation late one night three years ago, she'd told him the exact opposite about herself. He'd been lying in the dark on his bed, staring at the shadowy ceiling above him. Her voice had been a bare, vulnerable whisper along the phone line.

"I have some ugly things in my past, Gray. I don't just hop into bed with guys on a whim. Not anymore."

"You won't get any pressure from me, sweetheart. I'm quite

happy waiting for you." He meant that. He was an old fash-
ioned kind of guy at heart, and he'd fallen for her. Hard. Mad-
die was worth waiting for.

"Thank you." She drew a shuddering breath, a nervous
tremor to her voice as she spoke again. "I was a lot more carefree
in college. I went to a lot of frat parties, enjoyed my sexuality.
But I got hurt. These days, I have to trust a man before I'll even
think about sex."

Grayson shook off the memory, refocused on the computer in front of him and set his fingers to the keys. Fun and
flirty was definitely the way to go. He hoped she'd understand how he meant his next comment, that he attempted to
set her at ease.

BookNerd: No fair evading the question. ;)

MadHatter3000: Do you?

BookNerd: 5 days a week like a good boy.

Working out was where all his excess energy went. On
days when he couldn't forget her, when the need to storm
her apartment and force her to listen made him crazy, because his life was empty without her, he went to the gym.
Pushing his muscles to the limit left his mind blissfully
blank. Nights and weekends, however, were harder. Even the
pull of a good book lately couldn't drag his mind from the
fact that Maddie essentially lived right around the corner.
Her apartment downtown was ten minutes from here, five
in good traffic.

He typed in an additional message, aiming once again for
a playful tease. Hell, it had worked so far.

BookNerd: Would you like proof?

MadHatter3000: lol No pictures. I'm new to this and that's an aspect I'm not quite ready for. Yet.

He hadn't meant it that way, but now he was curious.

BookNerd: May I ask why now?

MadHatter3000: Because I'm 28. I'm not getting any younger, and this is . . . safe. It's been a while for me. A relationship ended badly. Christina was right when she told you I don't trust easily. But I'll admit I hate being alone. This is kind of a first step.

Grayson sat back, dropping his hands to his sides. His chest tightened with regret. That he'd hurt her had haunted him every day of the last three years. He hated knowing he'd hurt her to the point she'd shut down.

This time, his reply was a whole lot more honest.

BookNerd: You're not alone there. It's been a while for me, too. And for the record, I won't be sending any of those types of pics. The first time you see a certain part of my anatomy I'd rather it be up close and personal.

MadHatter3000: Cock. You can say it. I'm a noob, not a virgin.

He could only shake his head. She was softness and strength, boldness and shyness all rolled into one dynamite package, and he was happily struggling to keep up with her. When she tossed comments like that at him—the bold ones—said part of his anatomy throbbed to life again. His cock happily reminded him how long it had been since he'd held a woman in his arms, let alone made love to one. Oh, he'd tried. The first year after their breakup, he was so hurt by the way she'd iced him out, he was determined to forget her.

Except no woman could ever measure up. Phone sex with Maddie was miles better than actual sex with anyone else.

He'd given up attempting to date over a year ago. How the hell he was supposed to move on with his life when all he wanted was her?

His heart hung heavy, all those things he should have said to her a long time ago rising like a typhoon over his head.

Grayson sighed. How the hell did she want him to answer that? Playful was the way to go. If he didn't, he'd be doing everything he shouldn't. All unburdening himself would do was re-erect that wall between them, which would only serve to put him back where he'd already been—alone and without her.

BookNerd: All right, cock. Happy now?

MadHatter3000: That depends. Are you actually hard or just a tease?

He closed his eyes and forced himself to draw a shaky breath. Christ. She was going to kill him. He'd die a slow, painful death from lack of oxygen to the brain.

He opened his eyes and shook his head as he punched in a reply.

BookNerd: You're killing me here, you know that? Both. I find you intriguing. You're bolder than I expected. I expected you to shut me down by now. So I'll admit I'm pushing my luck, because your reactions tell me a lot about you and what you expect. From me and from this.

That, sadly, was the truth. He'd also said it because he was dying to know how she'd respond. He'd missed this, the hot, intimate chats.

MadHatter3000: Maybe this is exactly what I want and why I agreed to it.

Ah, now they were getting somewhere.

BookNerd: You want to step outside your box.

MadHatter3000: I want something hot and frivolous that doesn't end in heartbreak.

Grayson ignored the twinge of regret tightening in his gut and typed in a playful response. He had to play this cool. He was supposed to be a stranger to her.

BookNerd: Ditto. That was three questions, BTW. That's going to cost you.

MadHatter3000: Ok. I suppose you earned it. Lay 'em on me.

BookNerd: Now it's your turn. Are you aroused?

MadHatter3000: I'm getting warmer. Next?

He smiled. Damn tease.

BookNerd: That's all I get? Just warm?

MadHatter3000: Sorry, cowboy, but you're going to have work harder than that. ;)

Damn it all to hell. Now, he couldn't resist. He ought to, but he couldn't.

BookNerd: Tease. ;) Tell me what you're wearing.

MadHatter3000: You aren't going to ask what I look like?

Crap. He'd forgotten that. *Think fast, Lockwood.*

BookNerd: I already did and you didn't answer. I took the hint. Whatever you're comfortable with.

MadHatter3000: I'm a natural redhead.

And gorgeous. Maddie's copper locks flowed down her back in thick waves. She had the complexion to match, smooth, creamy skin and freckles that dotted her nose and cheeks.

BookNerd: I'd rather discover the truth of that for myself, thank you. ;)

MadHatter3000: lol I'm not sending a pic.

BookNerd: Did I ask for one?

MadHatter3000: Next question, please.

BookNerd: What. Are. You. Wearing?

Grayson sat back, glancing over the fast-paced conversation, and grinned. Christ, he'd missed her. Playful banter like this was what had originally brought them together three years ago. They'd gotten to know each other as colleagues and slowly over the year and a half he'd worked undercover at Bradbury, an easy friendship had formed. A work-related e-mail had somehow blossomed. She'd toss a subtle flirt at him. He'd respond and send her one back. It had launched a million small conversations between them, each one bolder than the last.

Another lengthy silence followed. This one so long he feared he really had pushed her beyond her comfort zone. Insides twisted in nervous, highly aroused knots, he set his laptop aside and surged to his feet, pacing to the windows again. The night around him was as quiet and serene as the rocking of the dock the house sat on. This view was what had made him purchase this house. Only now it did nothing for his scattered nerves. Christ. By time the she was done with him, he'd need a cold shower.

He counted fifteen ticks of the clock before his laptop pinged behind him. He turned his head, reading her reply from across the room.

MadHatter3000: Just my pj's.

He stared for a moment, stunned. *I'll be damned.* She'd actually told him. He moved to his computer and punched in a reply. The last time he'd been this aroused, an innocent chat with her had turned into something hot and delicious. That was the first time he discovered the sounds she made when she came.

BookNerd: Describe them.

MadHatter3000: t-shirt and panties.

BookNerd: I find that incredibly sexy.

Christ, she had no idea. Maddie had curves, a petite, perfect figure. The thought of her sitting over there in little more than one of those form hugging T-shirts she was fond of and a pair of panties had his cock swelling further, pressing painfully against his zipper. He reached down to readjust it into a more comfortable position.

BookNerd: Here's where all those probing questions are going to cost you.

MadHatter3000: LOL. Still not sending you a pic.

BookNerd: Take them off.

She didn't answer immediately. He tapped his finger on his laptop as he waited.

MadHatter3000: Panties?

BookNerd: All of it. Then tell me how you feel.

Chapter Three

Had she completely lost her mind?

Maddie dropped her shaking hands onto the sofa beside her and sank back into the cushions, staring at her laptop screen. Every limb seemed to be shaking. His words taunted her with what she wanted so badly she could taste it. Flirting with him was easy. Dave was sexy, in a subtle kind of way. She had to admit, her panties were already damp and her clit throbbed with the promise of the night. The idea that someone else would help her achieve orgasm was a lure she couldn't resist. Tonight, at least, she didn't feel so alone. Hannah was right. There was something addicting about that.

Except her mind had gotten stuck on the doing part. The thought of taking her clothes off had an ultra-vulnerable sensation twisting through her. She'd told him nothing but the truth earlier. This wasn't like her. In fact, she'd only done this kind of thing with one other man. Grayson.

Grayson Lockwood was the first man to get past her defenses, and look where that had gotten her? Which was exactly why she was here. This *wasn't* like her. Oh, she'd tried once or twice, but every single time she got close, she got cold feet. Since her assault, she'd never been able to make it past kissing. Having sex with someone always came down to one point: could she trust the man she was with? The answer had always been no. Sadly, she'd learned the hard way that she couldn't trust Grayson, either.

Hannah might be a diehard romantic, but she was right about one thing. Maddie was lonely, and it ate at her. Now that her two best friends had found their other halves, she yearned to find the same thing. For all her bravado, deep down, she was a little girl with a heart full of impossible dreams of Cinderella and Prince Charming.

Neither was she ready for another relationship. No, what she needed was something in the middle. Which meant, if she wanted company after the auction, she had to go *all* in. No matter how nervous she felt.

Besides, she really did like this guy. He was nice. Talking to him somehow set her at ease.

She gave a firm nod and sat up straight. *You can do this.*

Before she could decide what to do or say, another message popped onto her screen.

BookNerd: Nervous?

Maddie sighed. God, how did he do that? She must look like a ninny....

MadHatter3000: A little.

BookNerd: Me, too. My heart is hammering. We don't have to do this, you know. We could end it here and say goodnight.

The answer to that came as easily as her next breath. If she ended it here, she'd regret it.

MadHatter3000: I don't want to end it. I'm just nervous.

Of course, her mind now filled with uncertainties and questions she shouldn't ask. She stuffed her finger into her mouth, biting down on the short nail. What she liked about him was his honesty, but this particular question was of the "uncertain of herself and completely not sexy" variety. She had to ask, though, if only to put it out there.

MadHatter3000: Is it a turn-off? Am I ruining this?

That had to be one of the most vulnerable things she'd admitted to a man. It was right up there with the night she'd confessed her past to Grayson.

BookNerd: No. It's natural. Truth is, part of me is wondering if you think I'm pushing.

MadHatter3000: Are you?

Because he'd asked, and now she had to know.

BookNerd: Not intentionally. I find this arousing as hell. You're straight up with me, about who you and what you want. And I can't seem to help myself. But I don't want to give you the wrong impression, either.

MadHatter3000: You're not. TBH, your honesty is nice.

BookNerd: :) I'm glad. Ask me anything.

MadHatter3000: May I ask what you're wearing?

BookNerd: Same thing I wore to work today. I haven't changed yet. Shirt and slacks.

MadHatter3000: Tie?

BookNerd: Nope. That baby comes off the minute I get into my car at the end of the night. ;)

This discovery sent little flutters of excitement pulsing through her. Her panties were positively wet now. God, he was a corporate man. There was something so damned sexy about a man in a full suit.

She yearned to ask him what he did for a living but held back. The truth was, she had no desire to get to know him beyond what she needed for their date. She wasn't even sure if she wanted this to go beyond the one date. He intrigued her, though. That he was sitting over there, still fully dressed, told her a lot about him.

BookNerd: Would it help if I went first?

Her shoulders slumped, and she released the breath she wasn't aware of holding. God bless the man for his patience.

MadHatter3000: Yes. Please.

BookNerd: Ok. What would you like me to take off?

Maddie leaned back, tapping her fingers on her laptop, but the answer entered her thoughts seconds later. That was too easy.

MadHatter3000: The shirt. I like chests. If you workout as much as you say, I imagine you have a nice one.

BookNerd: Would you like proof?

Maddie stuffed a nail into her mouth, heart thumping like an out of control jackhammer. Did she? Hands down. She had almost a fetish with men's' chests. Of all the places on a man's body she found sexy, that one topped the list. A broad chest and well defined pecs and shoulders could make her cream her panties. Did she actually have the guts to say yes, though?

MadHatter3000: I won't send you one in return.

BookNerd: I'm okay with that. I promise I won't ask for anything you're not comfortable with.

MadHatter3000: Thanks. Can I ask you something?

BookNerd: You can ask me anything.

Maddie bit her bottom lip. She shouldn't. He'd already told her he'd rather the first time she see him naked to be in person, but that naughty part of her was dying to know....

MadHatter3000: If I asked you to send me a pic of your cock...would you?

BookNerd: Damn. You with the questions. You're killing me. Honestly. LOL Do you want one?

MadHatter3000: Would you?

BookNerd: No. ;)

She grinned. Damn it, she couldn't help it. She had to hand it to him. His confession meant for all intents and purposes, he was old fashioned like her. God, that was sexy, if only because it was so rare. She'd tried dating after she broke it off with Grayson, but that she wouldn't sleep with them meant most guys never made it past the first date.

MadHatter3000: LOL Now who's the tease?

BookNerd: Honestly?

MadHatter3000: Please. My nerves are shot.

BookNerd: Are you trembling?

Maddie stared at the screen. His intimate question sent her mind spiraling off in another direction. It was just words, yet her mind easily envisioned the way they'd leave his mouth. Soft, spoken on a husky murmur. She'd bet he had a bedroom voice. Smooth and velvety. Just the thought had her stomach flip-flopping and her clit pulsing.

She reached down, easing the throbbing between her thighs by stroking her slit through her panties, typing an awkward, one-handed response.

MadHatter3000: Yes.

BookNerd: God, I love that. It's a big turn on when a woman trembles in my arms. But the first time you see my cock, I want you close enough to touch it. I want to be able to feel your hand wrap around me.

Oh God, that did it. He was so damned laidback and subtle that all these little sexual tidbits he tossed at her hit their intended target...zinging straight to her core. No sooner had she read the words than the thought filled her mind. Wrapping her hand around his length as she stroked him. What did his cock look like? Was he long? Thick?

She found her clit through her panties and rubbed, allowing herself the moment. The pleasure that would wash over his features, though, was the ultimate. That. That's what she missed the most about sex, what she'd enjoyed about her carefree days in college—her partner's pleasure. What she craved, in the darkness of night when even B.O.B. couldn't satisfy the throbbing in her clit? A partner. A hot guy who made her cream her panties and who'd put his hands and his cock all over her. She wanted the luscious feel of his warm skin against hers. His hard cock sliding in and out of her. And she wanted to watch his face when his orgasm claimed him, to hear what he sounds he made. Did Dave groan softly? Or tremble quietly?

Yeah, when Hannah had told her she was having an online fling, Maddie had understood the need.

BookNerd: Tell me what you want, baby.

This, too, got her. *Baby*. A term of endearment filled with inherent intimacy. All it did was fill her mind with more fantasies. Of him whispering the words in her ear. The fantasy wrapped around her like a lure, and before she'd made the conscious decision, her fingers were typing out the word.

MadHatter3000: Ok.

Hands trembling, she sat back. She prayed he knew what she meant, because she wasn't sure she had the nerve to say it.

BookNerd: Give me a sec.

Nervous and edgy, Maddie set her laptop aside and stood, then crossed to the front windows and closed the blinds. Goose bumps shivered across her skin, and her stomach churned. She was alone in her own living room for crying out loud, but vulnerability still wrapped around her like a shroud. She could do this. She wanted this. Right?

Her laptop pinged moments later, and she turned her head. Standing out on her screen was a picture. In it, he appeared to be seated on a white couch, or perhaps a chair. He hadn't included his face. It was a picture from the neck to the waist, but it gave her an unprecedented view of his body.

She was sure her mouth had to be hanging open or that drool dripped off her chin, because for a moment, all she could do was stare. He had strong, thick shoulders and beefy pecs. The muscles of his abdomen were well-defined without being body builder obnoxious. His biceps were firm and well rounded. Oh, yeah. Christina definitely had good taste.

He also had a tattoo. A beautiful orange and gold phoenix covered his left pectoral muscle, rising out of orange flames and gray ash. One wing disappeared over the top of his shoulder, no doubt spilling down his shoulder blade. The tail ran down his arm. It stood out on his tanned skin, yet it wasn't flashy. The phoenix stood for rebirth, rising from the ashes. The thought of which did nothing but fill her with an overwhelming need to know the story behind it.

Pulled by the power of him, she moved to the couch and sat, her fingers trembling with a heady dose of arousal. Her head filled with erotic visions of him. If Dave were here, she could definitely see herself climbing that hot body....

MadHatter3000: Not bad.

BookNerd: lol Do I meet with your approval?

MadHatter3000: You'll do. ;) May I ask another question?

BookNerd: Ask away.

Maddie hesitated, her fingers hovering over the keyboard. Memories flooded her mind. Similar chats with Grayson…Lonely nights when she'd been too shy to tell him, too, what she wanted. He'd coaxed them out of her gently with a husky, *"Tell me what you're wearing, baby…"*

She shook off the memories and refocused on the picture. He wasn't Grayson.

MadHatter3000: Are your nipples sensitive?

BookNerd: Very.

Maddie stifled a groan. Drawn in by him, by the intimacy of the moment, of the question, her fingers kept typing. God, this was too easy. Surely that had to be a bad sign.

MadHatter3000: I love a man with sensitive nipples. Do you like them licked, sucked, pinched…?

BookNerd: Yes. ;) It's your turn, sweetheart. Shirt. Off, please.

Maddie stared at the screen. Heat shivered across the surface of her skin. How was it that such a simple demand could be so sexy? Was this what Hannah had meant? What she'd had with Cade? Maddie had to admit it was arousing as hell. Such a simple thing yet so…powerful. Her nipples tightened almost painfully, aching for the stroke of his fingers, which drew up images of his hands. They weren't showing in the picture. Were they smooth and soft? Or rough with callouses?

Mind made up, she set her laptop aside and stood. She could do this. Gripping her T-shirt by the hem, she whipped it off her head and dropped it the floor at her feet. Cool air rushed over her skin, and an ultra-vulnerable sensation twisted through her. She sat again and reached for her keyboard. It wasn't like he could see her, but that's what it felt like. Like she was getting naked in front of a lover for the first time.

MadHatter3000: Ok.

BookNerd: God, do you know how sexy that is? And? How do you feel?

MadHatter3000: Honestly? Feels a little strange sitting here by myself, half naked.

BookNerd: You're not alone, sweetheart. I'm right here with you.

God, how she wished he was….

MadHatter3000: May I ask what you're doing? Are you…

She couldn't bring herself to finish the sentence. It wasn't like she'd never done this before, but it still seemed too bold to ask a relative stranger.

BookNerd: Stroking myself? I'll admit I've rubbed myself through my pants, but no. It would be rude to start without you. ;) It's killing me, because I can't help imagining that patch of red curls between your thighs. I want to bury my face there and taste you. Inhale your aroma and stroke that sopping pussy with my tongue. You wet, sweetheart?

Oh God. At the thought, liquid heat curled through her, settling in the exact spot he'd mentioned. To have his mouth between her thighs, lapping at her. Her clit pulsed, throbbing and begging for release. She reached down, stroking herself through her panties again. She had to admit it. The thought of him over there, doing what she was, occasionally rubbing his cock because he was so aroused he couldn't help himself, provided a luscious lure.

She typed in a response with trembling fingers.

MadHatter3000: My panties are drenched. And I'm doing the same thing, stroking myself through my panties.

BookNerd: How's it feel?

MadHatter3000: Not as good as your tongue would.

BookNerd: You're killing me. LOL Tell me what you want me to do, sweetheart.

The term of endearment ought to feel too intimate, strange, yet somehow, it didn't. It made him feel familiar and relaxed her shaky nerves. It meant for all intents and purposes, he really did understand where her head was right then. The need for this vied with the part of her that was flat out scared to death. He had patience, and she appreciated that. More than she could tell him.

MadHatter3000: Get naked with me.

As she waited, thoughts of him filled her head. Standing before her, pulling off his clothing. She scrolled up the page, looking at his picture again, soaking in the sight of him. He had a fantastic body. Were his thighs as muscular as the rest of him? She bet he had a firm, round ass. Which did nothing but fill her head with visions of him looming over her, that hard body pressing her into the mattress.

The fingers of her left hand found her breast, stroking and circling the distended nipple as she let herself get lost in the fantasy. Her legs locked around his lean hips, his cock pumping into her. God, she missed that, the feel of a man's body against her and inside her, in a way that was natural, an extension of an intimate relationship, instead of constantly connected to a terrifying moment....

When she was sure she was leaving a wet spot on her couch, or that she'd start without *him*, her laptop pinged with an incoming message. She refocused on the screen.

BookNerd: Done. Your turn, baby. Take those panties off.

A hot little shiver fluttered through her. That meant he was naked, sitting at his computer waiting for her.

She set her laptop aside and slid her panties to the floor. Fully naked now and trembling in earnest, with need and nerves, she resumed her seat.

MadHatter3000: Done. Are you still hard?

BookNerd. Are you getting any warmer?

MadHatter3000: No fair answering a question with a question. ;) Actually, I've been wet and throbbing since you asked me to take my clothes off.

BookNerd: Ahh, so you ARE aroused by this.

MadHatter3000: I've been staring at your picture, stroking my nipples. I feel very sexy sitting here, talking to you. You make me feel comfortable.

BookNerd: I'm honored. And yes. To answer your question, I'm hard enough to hammer nails. The thought of you naked over there does the same thing to me. Tell me what you want, baby.

Maddie sighed. Another question that was all too easy to answer.

MadHatter3000: In a perfect world? You'd be here, and your tongue would be buried inside me. Now? I want you to make me cum. Make me see stars, Dave.

Make me forget....

Chapter Four

Maddie stared at the contents of the small box in front of her. The bookshop was quiet, only the sound of the rain and the traffic out on the street cutting the silence. She'd been sorting through a box of used books when the package arrived via a small, Priority Mail Flat Rate box. The note on top wasn't signed, but she didn't need to ask to know who it was from. Dave had sent her a gift.

A week and a half had passed since she'd received her first message from him. They'd chatted every night since, and every night, he left her breathless, more sated than she'd been in a long time, and usually falling to sleep with a grin as wide as Montana. She had to admit she liked him. He was sexy, in a subtle, take-charge kind of way. They didn't talk much about jobs or life beyond "how was your day?" Which was okay with her. She had no desire to get to know him beyond what they had. This was exactly what she needed—a hot, uncomplicated fling that would propel her into moving on with her life. To forget Grayson Lockwood and her assault in college.

The auction was in three days. The thought of meeting him in person had her tied in knots, but Hannah was right. She couldn't stay single and celibate forever. The thought of finally having sex again filled her with equal parts desire and dread. Oh, the need was there. The thought of his cock sliding inside of her made her clit throb. She was dying to see him up close and personal, to get her hands all over him. If he was as good in person as he was online, she wouldn't be able to walk the next day.

The thought of sex, though, had memories rising over her. Along with them came the anxiety. The last time she'd tried to have sex with a man—the healthy, natural kind—the touch of his hand as it slid beneath her top had sent her right back to that night in college. It was a step she wanted to take. She needed to leave the past where it belonged, once and for all, but whether or not she'd able to go through with it was another matter. Could she truly trust that she was safe now and have a hot little fling with Dave, like the ones she'd had back in college, before her assault had filled her with fear? She wouldn't know until the moment arrived.

One thing she did know: she didn't want a relationship. She needed to take things one step at a time, and that was one she wasn't ready for. This morning's gift, however, had complicated written all over it. That he was sending her gifts told her in no uncertain terms he wanted more than sex. The thought had her stomach caught somewhere between giddy butterflies and terrified tangles.

The bell on the door to the shop dinged, announcing an incoming customer, and Maddie set the box aside and lifted her gaze. Hannah strode through, a bright smile lighting up her face and Cade in tow, with baby Emily tucked in one beefy arm. The sight of the baby had her mood immediately lifting. It had been a whole two weeks since Maddie had seen her.

Disregarding this morning's surprise for the moment, she squealed, clapped her hands in glee and all but skipped around the counter.

"Ohhh, you brought the baby." She bypassed Hannah and headed straight for Cade and the cuteness lounging on his shoulder.

Hannah laughed softly as she whizzed past. "I asked Cade to bring her down. I knew you'd love to see her."

Hannah was right. Emily was three months old and sweet and perfect, and Maddie adored her. She, Hannah, and Christina got together at least once a month, often once a week for lunch or a movie and wine night, but there never seemed enough time to visit with the baby.

Maddie winked at Cade as she plucked the adorable little bundle out of his arms. "Thanks for bringing my baby to see me, hot stuff."

"Hot Stuff" was a playful nickname she'd given him when he and Hannah were dating. It was exactly what he was—tall, broad-shouldered gorgeousness. Hannah called him GQ. A rich, corporate lawyer, the man was what Hannah had always jokingly called "a fellow geek." The two of them were peas in a pod, both into books and research, but Cade didn't look the part. He had the looks of a cover model.

As she clutched the baby to her chest, Cade let out a quiet laugh. "My pleasure entirely, Miss O'Riley. You know, you should think of getting one of your own, though."

Cade winked at her, and Maddie couldn't resist a grin. Teasing him came too easily, but the impossibility of his suggestion swirled around her and clutched at her chest.

"Oh, no. I'm not ready for one of my own yet." Maddie set the baby into the crook of her left arm and gazed down at her. "You do make such pretty babies, though, Cade."

Emily had a full head of thick, dark hair like her father, and big wide eyes, and she smelled heavenly, like baby powder and sweetness. She wasn't fussy, either, but content to let people pass her around—so long as she had a shoulder to lounge on. Every time Maddie saw her, her heart gave that impossible little twinge. Okay, so she'd admit it. She wanted this. The whole fairytale, what these two had found. What Christina and Sebastian had found. A man who'd love her in spite of all her weird little quirks, and she wanted a yard full of pretty, red-haired babies to go with him.

"Besides." She sighed. "That would require Prince Charming to actually have my address. I think he's gotten lost."

It didn't help, of course, that her heart still hung onto the one man she'd never have, which was pathetic, considering three years had passed since he'd walked out of her life. Or rather, let her go.

She didn't have to ask to know what Hannah would say

about the matter. *"Would you do it again, if you could?"* Hannah had asked her that once, referring, of course, to her decision to end her relationship with Grayson.

The conversation had begun because Hannah had contemplated an affair with Cade. Hannah had been as scared as Maddie was now, afraid of falling in love. Maddie had told her to go for it or she'd regret it, because Maddie had a heart full of regrets. None of which she knew what to do with. The day she'd found that article on the front page of a local newspaper, her heart had sunk. She'd been so angry and so hurt; she'd left Grayson at that romantic little cabin all by himself. She'd stood him up. Back then, though, she'd been so sure she'd made the right decision.

Now? Not so much. Her mind filled with "what-if's." What if she'd gone? What if she'd given him a chance to explain? Would things have turned out differently?

Except now she was stuck. How did she move on when she wasn't sure she'd made the right decision? When it was too late to do anything about it anyway? When she was sure she'd met the man she'd wanted to marry, only to discover he wasn't who he said he was? That he'd essentially lied his way into her bed?

Okay, so she hadn't slept with Grayson. They'd shared a hell of a lot, though. She'd shared things with him she didn't tell just anybody. So while she couldn't deny she had regrets, the sense of betrayal went deep, and she didn't know how to get over that or let it go.

"Oh, I'll bet Prince Charming's closer than you think."

Cade's odd comment, and the *I've got a secret* tone to

his voice had Maddie glancing up. As if his words weren't enough of a puzzle, he grinned at her, something mysterious working behind his eyes.

"Cade!"

Behind her, Hannah let out a hushed reprimand, and Maddie turned sideways to peer at her. Her best friend glared none-too-subtly at her husband, but at Maddie's look her frown tipped into an awkward smile. Okay, she'd known Hannah long enough to know she couldn't hide a secret if she tried. Hannah was too honest. Despite her impassive expression, her best friend had a worried, shifty look about her. The same look Christina often got when discussing Maddie's blind date to the auction.

Cade laughed, light-hearted and dismissive, and shook his head, holding up his hands in mock surrender. "I just meant you shouldn't give up hope. Look at me. I'd given up on women altogether before Hannah waltzed her way into my life." Cade winked at her. "You never know."

He breezed past Maddie to Hannah, hooked an arm around her waist and tugged her against his side. Maddie could only stare for a moment, suspicion itching at the edges of her consciousness. Why did the two of them look like they knew something she didn't? Despite their intimate embrace, Hannah still sent her husband an, albeit subtle, warning glare.

What on earth was with her friends these days? They all seemed as if they shared a secret somebody had forgotten to tell *her*.

Maddie shook off the sensation and arched a brow at

Cade. "Aren't you usually at the office this time of day?"

Cade turned toward her, one arm wrapped around Hannah's back, and nodded. "Mmm. I've taken the morning off. Too many hours at the office leaves little time for Em when she's awake. So, I'm taking a half day to spend some Daddy time with my girl."

Because he was a lawyer, Cade's profession often meant long hours were the rule, not the exception. Hannah had told her once he usually wasn't home before seven. Maddie was glad to see he was taking time for the baby.

Cade smiled, crossed the space to her, and held out his arms. "Now, if you'll kindly hand back my baby, my daughter and I have a date."

Maddie offered a reluctant but playful sigh. "If you insist." She bent her head, inhaling the sweet baby powder scent that clung to the child, kissed her forehead, then set her into his waiting hands. "Have fun, Dad."

He tucked Emily gently in the crook of an arm nearly twice as long as she was. "Oh, I plan on it." He glanced up then, flashing a teasing grin, his green eyes alight with amusement. "I hear you've got yourself a date."

Maddie's cheeks grew warm. She shook her head. "I don't even want to know what she's told you."

"Just the basics, Maddie, I promise." Hannah offered a gentle smile.

Despite the reassurance, Maddie sighed. "I have to admit I'm nervous. It's the first real date I've had in a while."

"Word of advice? Enjoy it. Best damn thing I ever did." He didn't give her time to respond, but turned to Hannah again and bent, murmuring against her mouth as he kissed her. "I'll leave her with Mom, probably around eleven or so. I might be late tonight."

When Hannah lifted onto her toes to kiss him back, Maddie turned away, giving them some privacy. She ran her fingers over the top of the small box. Dave's present was a book, one of her favorites. *Poems* by Emily Dickinson. It was a sweet gesture.

Cade left the store, the door chime dinging behind him.

Hannah stepped up beside her, peering around her shoulder. "What's this?"

Warmth bloomed in Maddie's chest as she slid the box in Hannah's direction. "I got a surprise this morning. The mailman dropped it off just before you guys got here. Take a peek. I have to admit, he outdid himself on this one."

Hannah turned her head, a pleased grin curling across her face. "I take it you like him."

Maddie turned to the box instead. She wasn't sure she wanted to discuss the details. If she did, she might talk herself out of this. "I'll admit it. He's…nice. We've been talking just about every night."

She reached into the box and pulled out the note, releasing a heavy, melancholic sigh as she read it again.

I'm enjoying getting to know you, Maddie. Came across this and thought of you.

It was a completely sentimental gift, and she had to admit, she wasn't immune to its charm. She had a penchant for romantic poetry, in large part due to her grandpa. Her grandfather had raised her from the time she was small. She didn't have any memories of her parents. Missionaries who'd traveled the world, they'd left her with her grandparents when she was three, only to die a few years later in a horrible accident. A fire of all things. Grandma had died twenty years ago now, Grandpa only about five.

She had so many memories of him reading with her. He'd had a stack of books much like the ones Hannah had—old, weathered favorites he'd kept on a small shelf in the living room, and every night he'd read to her. Despite his years in the states, his Irish lilt had never quite faded, and if she closed her eyes the sound of his voice came as clear as it had then. She'd always treasured those books. They were like comfort food, something she reverted to when stressed, because they filled her with good memories. To get a copy of a book she knew practically by heart was an overwhelming gesture. The question was, what had made him choose this particular book? Had Christina mentioned it to him? Or was it simply a happy coincidence?

"Wow, Madds." Hannah reached inside the box and carefully lifted out the book, opened the hardback cover and peered at the title page.

The tan dust jacket was slightly weathered with age, and the green spine had slight fraying on the corners, but otherwise, it was in excellent condition. This book had been cared for.

Hannah turned to look at her. "This is a really thoughtful gift."

Maddie laughed softly and shook her head. "I know. He's good. I'll give him that."

Hannah set the book back into the box and quirked a quizzical brow, her eyes lit up and gleaming, as pleased as a cat with a bowl full of cream. "So. I take it this book means things are going *well*?"

Maddie didn't miss Hannah's subtle reference. She might have blushed, but she couldn't drum up the emotion. After all, she'd taken her cue from Hannah and Cade. She knew darn well her best friend had "been there, done that."

"They are. He's sweet and sexy as hell. Did you know he has a tattoo? A gorgeous phoenix on his left shoulder." She ached to be close enough to touch it one day, the very thought of which was a tangle of emotion caught in her chest. Nervousness and arousal, excitement and dread. The first time he touched her, she'd probably jump out of her skin.

"No, I didn't know he had a tattoo. Christina never mentioned it." Something vaguely suspicious flitted across Hannah's features, there and gone. Hannah flashed another teasing grin. "I guess that means he's sent you pictures? You know what he looks like, then?"

"I didn't see his face. Only certain parts of him." This time, fierce heat slid up Maddie's neck into her cheeks. She laughed and jabbed a pointed finger at Hannah. "And that's all the details you're getting."

Hannah laughed and held up her hands. "I won't ask. Though I am glad you're having a good time." Hannah bumped her shoulder. "It's good to see you happy, Madds."

Maddie smiled, warmth blooming in her chest. "Ditto. I have to admit, though, the thought of meeting him has my nerves scattered. There are only three days until the auction, before I have to meet him in person. I don't want any more than something casual, but this gift has complicated written all over it."

Hannah slung an arm around her shoulders and squeezed. "I'm going to quote a very wise woman I know, who once told me the same thing. It's just a date, Madds. If you're lucky, you'll get some hot sex with a guy who clearly toots your horn. It doesn't have to be any more than that. Stop thinking and enjoy it."

Maddie shook her head. "I hope you're right, Han. I really do. 'Cause three years is long enough."

Her phone pinged from where it sat on the counter, and Maddie's heart picked up speed.

Hannah nudged her with an elbow. "Hot sex, Madds. The sweaty, wake up the next morning sore and exhausted kind. It's a good thing. You can do this. But if you don't go for it, you'll never get it."

Maddie turned her head and cocked a brow. Okay, so it was T.M.I., but she had to know. Curiosity and all that. "Wake up sore? Seriously? When?"

Hannah flushed to the roots of her hair but giggled. "Those first few months after Cade moved back to Seattle. You have to experience it once in your life to realize how glorious it is."

Maddie could only stare for a moment before a grin bloomed. "And to think you were the shy one."

Yeah, okay, so she was jealous of her best friend. She wanted that, the freedom and joy of loving someone. The thought only reinforced what she already knew. She could do this. She wanted this. Right? Which meant she had to take that step. Out of her box and into…his.

With trembling fingers, she picked up her phone and brought up her Gchat. As expected, the message was from Dave.

BookNerd: I sent you something. Please let me know when you get it.

Hannah flashed a bright smile then moved around behind the counter, busying herself with the inventory sheets Maddie had set out earlier.

Maddie drew a deep breath, staring down at her phone. Every body part seemed to be shaking, including her knees. God, here went nothing.

MadHatter3000: Just got here.

BookNerd: Oh, good. Do you like it?

Here's where she had to be honest with him. Hannah was right. Doing so usually settled her nerves.

MadHatter3000: It was very sweet. TY. But it's an intimate gift. I meant what I said. I don't want complicated. If ur hoping for more, I'm going to disappoint u.

That was almost rude to say to him, but it was the truth. She wanted sex, but she wasn't ready for anything serious. The question was, would this be the moment he backed out of their date?

BookNerd: Relax, babe. It's just a gift. I'm fond of surprises.

That was exactly what terrified her. Grayson had been, too. Their friendship back when had started much like this one, a text or an e-mail here and there. They'd eventually led to nights of lying in the dark listening to the sexy sound of his voice. She still had the bracelet he'd given her for her birthday three years ago. It was an extravagant thing, expensive for sure, but simple and beautiful. A thin gold chain with a round amethyst set in gold. It currently sat at the bottom of her panty drawer. She'd thought about pawning it, but hadn't been able to let it go. It was too sentimental and selling it seemed rude.

Dave's gift this morning left her with the same unsettled feeling. Look where her relationship with Grayson had gotten her. Was she insane for doing this?

When she didn't reply, because her stomach had twisted itself into a nervous knot and she couldn't think of what *to* say, another message popped onto her screen.

BookNerd: Look. I'm sorry if I made you uncomfortable. I happened to come across a copy, and I thought of you. Christina told me you owned a bookstore, and the book is a favorite. It's not any more complicated than that. You can send it back if it's too much. I hope our date still stands, though.

Regret tightened in Maddie's chest. Great. She'd offended him. His last statement, too, caught her, bringing up a whole slew of questions. Namely, was he actually worried she wouldn't still want to meet him? What did he expect from her? From this? This blind date had taken on a life of its own. She enjoyed the hell out of it for what it was, but this gift hinted at something else, something that only reminded her of the upcoming auction. At some point, she'd have to take her relationship with him offline and into reality. Was she ready for that?

Deciding she had to know, she typed in a quick response and hit send before she lost the nerve to ask.

MadHatter3000: Srry. Didn't mean to offend or sound ungrateful. It was very sweet, but r u hoping to get lucky?

The question was partly a tease, but she'd asked because his response would tell her what he expected. More to the point, it would tell her what *she* could expect.

BookNerd: You didn't offend. And yes. ;) Seriously? I enjoy you. I don't want to screw this up because of an impulsive decision. I have to go. Meeting in a few. Will I see you tonight?

Would he?

Yet even as she asked herself the question, the answer swelled inside of her. She would. Hannah was right. The flirting, the orgasms, their chats, were addicting. Now she had something that filled the empty silence of the night, something to look forward to besides her B.O.B. and her empty apartment when the lonely ache became unbearable.

And, okay, she couldn't deny it. She wanted more. She wanted something physical. She wanted him real and in front of her. The whole nine yards. His hands on her body, the taste of his breath as it mixed with hers, and his cock sliding into her. The thought had her knees shaking, but if she let this opportunity pass her by, she'd regret it. At some point, she had to leave the past where it belonged. So, she forced her shaking fingers to type in the response and hit send before she lost the nerve to do it.

MadHatter3000: C U 2night.

BookNerd: I'm glad. Later, baby.

When his name blipped off her screen, Maddie released a

breath filled with equal parts excitement and relief.

Hannah lifted her gaze from the papers and smiled. "See? Piece of cake. You can do this."

Maddie let loose a half-maniacal laugh. She was sure she sounded like she'd gone off the deep end, which summed up the emotions thrumming through her. "Oh yeah. Piece of cake, Han. Piece of cake."

Hannah abandoned the stack of papers and stepped to her side, wrapping her in a tight hug that reminded her too much of Christina. "It'll be okay, Madds. You'll see. Do you want this?"

Maddie let the tension drain from her shoulders. "Yes."

Hannah released her, the corners of her mouth tipped up in sympathy, and shook her head.

"Then swallow the fear and do it anyway. Let yourself have this. I was terrified the day I met Cade for the first time at The Space Needle. I was sure he'd take one look at me and go home. But he didn't. He took me in his arms and God, Madds. He had an erection hard enough to hammer train track spikes." Hannah giggled, then rolled her eyes in bliss. "But that first time…"

Maddie's mind filled with the fantasy of Dave drawing her against that big, hard chest. A heated shiver ran the length of her spine. "That good, huh?"

Hannah pursed her lips and nodded. "So much better in person. I understand the fear, though."

"Probably better than anyone." Maddie dropped her gaze to her sneakers and nodded. Hannah had been judged one too many times for the scars on her face. Some men were shallow, and she'd met too many of them. She'd been as terrified at the thought of taking her relationship with Cade into reality. At least Maddie wasn't alone in her fear.

"Your past doesn't make you who you are, so don't let it. Cade taught me that." Hannah hugged her again then released her. "Reach out and take this, Madds. Just because you can. You're twenty-eight, gorgeous, single and successful. Hold your head high. You deserve this. You owe it to yourself."

* * *

Later that night, Maddie sat staring at her computer. Waiting. That had to be pathetic, yet here she was, pretending to watch TV, her laptop seated on her knees. Their closer, J.J., had come in early, leaving Maddie plenty of time to anticipate tonight's conversation. Plenty of time to work herself into a frenzy of nerves. She'd had dinner already. The kitchen was clean and her laundry was done. There were a million other things she could be doing. Like watching the paranormal program she'd recorded on her DVR the other night. Or reading the book Dave had sent.

What was she doing, instead? Sitting here waiting for his Gchat name to appear online. When it actually did, her heart leapt, a full-out giddy little flip-flop. When his message popped up seconds later, her heart took off on a sprint, and her hands began to shake. God, that was pathetic. Not only had she waited for him, but she was so excited to see him she was coming out of her skin.

BookNerd: Hey

MadHatter3000: Hey

Despite the fact that they weren't even in the same room, awkward tension rose like a tangible object. She had no idea what to say to him. Their last conversation had been awkward at best. So, she sat and waited, stomach rolling with nausea.

It didn't take long for another message to pop up.

BookNerd: We okay?

We. His particular use of the word caught her and had her fear running away with itself. She didn't want a "we." What she wanted was something in the middle.

She sighed. She was caught somewhere between her inability to trust men and the future she ached to have, but it meant taking that first step and this was it.

MadHatter3000: We're ok. Sorry about earlier. You spooked me. Getting that gift made me wonder what you're expecting from this.

BookNerd: Am I hoping to get you naked at some point? Yes. ;) Otherwise? I'm not expecting anything. I'm afraid to tell you, sweetheart, I really am a geek. Books are my idea of seduction. It was my way of saying I like you. I'm looking forward to meeting you, you know. I hope you are, too.

Was she? Hands down. She hadn't had sex with a man in well over four years, an entire year before she'd met Grayson. She'd wanted to make love to him, but hadn't been able to because the fear had gotten to her, filling her mind with ugliness. Well, no more. She was tired of being alone. Maybe she wasn't ready to give out her heart yet. Of that she was certain. Maybe this thing with Dave would only be a fling, but with any luck, she'd find her feet again.

Decision made, she typed in another response.

MadHatter3000: I have to be honest as well. This? Online? Is easy, b/c it's simple. It's a fantasy. This I can do. But in person? The thought scares the crap out of me. It's been a while for me. I meant what I said. I'm not ready for more than this.

BookNerd: I'm not asking you for more. Though, I may ask you to take off your panties. ;) Would that be a yes, then? Are you looking forward to meeting at the auction?

That he'd repeated the question stood out to her and had her mind shifting gears. Was he afraid she *wasn't* looking forward to their date? It hinted that he was nervous, too. Not for the first time since she'd start chatting with him, seeing his human side eased the worry gnawing at her stomach.

MadHatter3000: Yes. My panties are damp. I've been waiting for you.

Heart still firmly seated in her throat, she added another message, as an afterthought.

MadHatter3000: That's pathetic, right?

BookNerd: If it is, I'm right there with you, baby. Getting to talk to you is the best part of my day.

Knowing that sent little butterflies dancing through her stomach. Like she was sixteen all over again, sitting in Tom Wilson's pickup, in the dark parking lot of that deserted park.

BookNerd: Relax, okay? We'll play it by ear. No pressure, I promise. I'm just looking forward to seeing you. I want you close enough to touch. Now ask me what I want to do to you when I see you. ;)

Maddie smiled. Now this she couldn't resist.

MadHatter3000: Let me guess, you plan to drag me off somewhere quiet to have your way w/ me?

BookNerd: Not quite. Thought I'd start with your mouth first. Maybe work my way down your neck…

Nerves eased, she relaxed into the sofa cushions and fell easily into the usual play.

MadHatter3000: I might actually let you. ;)

BookNerd: Baby, I'm hoping you'll let me do a whole lot more than kiss you. I want to feel you tremble in my arms when I find all those sensitive spots. I want to feel your breath on my neck when my fingers find you hot and wet…

And there it was. The single solitary statement to send her stomach right back into a riotous mass of anxious nerves. It was beyond pathetic to be twenty-eight and still acting like a virginal high school girl.

MadHatter3000: Dave?

BookNerd: Yeah?

MadHatter3000: I'm nervous.

BookNerd: Me too, baby. Me too.

Chapter Five

The name on his screen doused his libido like a bucket of ice water. Grayson sat staring at the word. The name Maddie had called him stood out on the page, all but lit up and blinking. So, that was the name Christina had given her. He supposed she'd had to tell Maddie something, but the name taunted him with what he wanted so damn bad he could taste it: to tell her who he really was.

Damn it. He slammed the lid shut, dropped his laptop onto the couch beside him with a little more force than intended, and surged to his feet. Pacing away from the couch, he dragged his hands through his hair. He hated lying to her. Oh for sure when she found out, she'd be pissed, but he'd waited three years for this chance. Three long damn years of trying to move on with his life, but not being able to. Because he missed her.

He needed her to know he hadn't hidden the truth to hurt her, that he hadn't intended for her to find out his real name the way she had. Damn it, he needed her to know the truth. Everything he would have told her that weekend, had she shown up.

It would mean eventually bearing an ugly, painful wound, though. He'd have to show her the scars on his back and share all those dark places. The things he'd spent sixteen years trying to forget. He still saw his father on occasion. He'd left home at thirteen, because living on the streets was better than living with an angry drunk, never knowing if he'd be safe going to sleep at night. Yet now that he'd gotten his life together, dear ol' dad would call or show up out of the blue, pretending everything was great. As if all those years of abuse hadn't happened. That the damn scars on his back didn't exist or he hadn't spent a year on the streets and not once had the man come searching for him.

"I don't care what you do with the little bastard…."

His father's words that long ago day rang in his head. That was the day Arthur had sought parental custody. Doing so had meant months in court and a restraining order, but in the end, his biological father hadn't contested.

The ping of an incoming instant message sounded from the vicinity of the couch behind him. Right. He'd left Maddie hanging. With a sigh, he resumed his seat and opened his laptop lid. A new message blinked out at him from the screen.

MadHatter3000: Did I scare you off?

For all her bravado and sass, deep down, Maddie had insecurities, like everybody else. It's what he loved so much about her. She was humble and honest.

And you're lying to her.

Guilt rose over him again, tightening his stomach, and for a moment, he could only stare at the screen. He hadn't meant for their chats to go this far. He'd only meant to draw her out of herself, for her to get to know him again. He couldn't back out now, though. Not without telling another lie, which would go against everything he wanted: to earn her trust. The only way for that to happen would be to act natural. Otherwise, she'd know something was up. This had to work. He couldn't lose her again.

BookNerd: Sorry. Had to get up for a minute. I'll quote somebody else I know. I don't scare so easily. ;)

MadHatter3000: Thought perhaps I was little too honest.

BookNerd: I like honesty. Truth is, my real name's not Dave. I wanted anonymity until we met at the auction. Tell me what you're doing.

MadHatter3000: I'm staring at you, actually. You're very yummy inspiration. I've started without you.

Grayson groaned, his cock twitching against his belly. He'd taken a huge chance by sending her that pic, on the off chance she'd recognize him somehow. His only saving grace was knowing she'd never seen him with his shirt off, a fact he'd made sure of up until now. Back then, she'd wanted to take things slow, and he'd been happy to let her, in part because he feared the scars on his back would disgust her. It hadn't happened yet with any of his previous lovers, but the fear was still there, nonetheless.

The thought of the conversation that would follow terrified him. Those were memories he only wanted to forget.

He'd moved so far beyond the terrified boy he'd once been, but he would carry the scars forever.

Those words from Maddie, though, were the entire reason he'd taken the chance.

BookNerd: God, you have no idea how much of a turn-on that is, to know you're over there with your fingers buried in your pussy, thinking about me. Exactly how wet are you, baby?

MadHatter3000: Very. It's all hot and slippery.

The image filled his mind, the way it had a thousand times before. Her, with her legs spread and her fingers buried in her heat. All those nights he laid in his bed, alone, listening to the sound of her ragged breathing as she stroked that hot pussy. He dropped his head back and closed his eyes, fisted his cock, and stroked slowly as the sounds she'd made long ago filled his head. By God, she was beautiful in the throes of passion. He ached to be a fly on the wall of her apartment.

When he didn't respond—because he couldn't make his brain work much past that image of her—another message popped up.

MadHatter300: Guys like to know that stuff, right?

His heart twisted at another sign of her insecurity.

BookNerd: Sorry. You distracted me for a minute. You make my cock ache, sweetheart. That's perfect.

MadHatter3000: You want me?

More memories flooded his mind. He squeezed the head of his cock, swiping his thumb over the bead of slick liquid dripping out the tip as the sound of her voice filled his head. She'd said those exact words to him once three years ago, had spoken them on a breathless, distracted whisper. Her voice had become an erratic, jerky huff that filled his mind with images of her long, slender fingers flying over her clit as she raced toward orgasm. It had taunted him then and did so again now.

BookNerd: You have no idea.

MadHatter3000: What r u thinking?

BookNerd: I'm imagining you, with your legs spread, fingers stroking your pussy. I bet you look incredible. Christ, I can almost smell you. I'd be on my knees at your feet, worshiping that pussy. I ache to replace those fingers with my tongue.

MadHatter3000: God, u don't know what that does to me...

He let out a soft curse and dropped his head back onto the sofa. His cock was so hard, so engorged, every stroke had extreme pleasure shooting to his toes. He was a sneeze from the edge. A couple of long strokes would be all it took. The imagined sound of her voice wrapped him like hot velvet, like she was there beside him, and another memory lodged itself in his mind. Another heated phone call, once upon a time. *"Tell me what you'd do to me, Gray..."*

Too ramped up and too damn close to imploding, he forced himself to open his eyes and released his cock, focusing, instead on the computer. If he didn't, he was going to come without her, and this wasn't about his needs. It was about hers. He could take care of himself later.

He thought for a minute, then dove into the fantasy.

BookNerd: I like it slow. I'd take my time with you. Caress your thighs, stroke your belly, pinch your nipples. I'd lean in and inhale your scent. I bet you smell incredible.

MadHatter3000: U like that?

God, did he ever.

BookNerd: A woman's scent is damn erotic. I'd have to lean in and taste. Long, slow strokes of my tongue, each one ending with a flick over your clit. I'd take my time, relishing the way you taste and the musk of your scent. Can you feel my tongue, baby?

MadHatter3000: God yes.

Grayson dragged a shaky hand through his hair. Christ. He could almost hear her moan that time. When she exploded, he'd no doubt go with her, and he wouldn't have to touch himself at all. Every inch of him was set to combust.

Encouraged, he continued, allowing himself to get lost in the fantasy, for her benefit.

BookNerd: I'd swirl my tongue around your clit, scrape my teeth over your mound, nibble the insides of your thighs, stroking your lips with my thumbs...touching everywhere but where you want me to.

MadHatter3000: Tease...

BookNerd: ;) All the while my hands are all over you. Caressing and massaging your breasts, twirling your nipples between my fingers. Are your nipples sensitive, sweetheart?

He knew they were, because she'd told him once, but for the sake of the charade, he'd asked. And because he ached to know what she'd tell him.

MadHatter3000: Mmm. Very. I like them pinched.

BookNerd: Do the opposite for me. Caress your fingers over them, lightly, like your tickling them.

Thirty seconds passed before her response popped up.

MadHatter3000: Gives me shivers and makes them harder...

He groaned.

BookNerd: I want to bite one.

MadHatter3000: Ohhh, I like that, the soft scrape of ur teeth. What would u do next? Don't stop.

Another memory lodged itself in his mind. She'd said that to him once him before, too. Her voice had been soft and trembling at the time. *"Don't stop, Gray...please don't stop."*

His fingers shook so much it took three tries to get his next message out.

BookNerd: Are you hot, baby?

MadHatter3000: Yessss. So close.

Grayson closed his eyes and dragged in a much needed breath. So was he. So close he was shaking. Every cell in his body was focused on her, to the point that the imagined sound of her voice filled his head. Every breath and sigh she no doubt made rang in his mind. He reached down, allowed himself a slow, luscious stroke of his cock, imagining her seated before him, thighs spread, chest heaving. God, this conversation was going to drive him out of his mind.

He released his aching cock, ignoring the urge to close his eyes and get lost in the fantasy she had swirling in his head, to allow himself the delicious orgasm hovering just beyond reach. Instead, he sat up, picked up his laptop and set it on his knees. *Focus, Lockwood. This is about her, not you.* He wanted her to trust him, to relax with him, and it started with something as simple as following her lead.

BookNerd: I'd dive in. Put my hands beneath your ass and pull you into my mouth, bury my face and my tongue in your pussy. Licking and sucking on your clit. Your hands would be in

my hair, your hips rocking to the rhythm as I flick my tongue back
and forth, like butterfly kisses . . .

She went silent then, and his head filled with more visions. Of her on her couch, exactly the way he'd
described—legs spread, fingers pumping in and out of herself. Abandoning the computer for the sake of pleasure.

So, he did the same, sat back, leisurely stroking his cock to
thoughts of her as he waited. When a full minute passed in
silence, though, the urge to know overrode everything else.
Damn it. He hated not being able to see her, or at the very
least, hear her.

BookNerd: Tell me what you're doing baby. Be my eyes . . .

MadHatter3000: I'm sorry. I'm so damn close. This isn't as
easy as I expected. If I type, I can't touch, but if I close my eyes
and enjoy, I have to ignore u . . .

Grayson let out a frustrated groan. Of all things for her to
say. God, she had no idea. What he wanted so badly he could
taste it was to call her. To let the sweet sound of her voice
wrap around him. Her voice always went soft and husky
when she was close to orgasm. He ached to tell her everything he was thinking, describe in detail all the things he
wanted to do her, the way he used to once upon a time. Because he knew. It would heat her up. She loved it when he
talked that way to her, had told him once it made her hot,
and he ached to take her over the edge.

BookNerd: Then don't. Stop replying and just enjoy. I'm right
there with you. Close your eyes and feel me beside you. Be my
hands, baby. Stroke that hot pussy for me.

MadHatter3000: Not fair . . .

BookNerd: Believe me, I'm getting just as much out of this as you are. Just imagining your pleasure, what you must look like.... Christ, you have me so damn hard.

MadHatter3000: Describe ur cock?

Grayson dropped his gaze to his lap, but couldn't help an ironic half grin. Now there was a question he'd never been asked. Maddie had never asked before. Leave it to her to push him out of the comfortable little box he kept himself in.

BookNerd: About six inches. Thick. The head is large and purple and it's leaking. All for you.

MadHatter3000: Mmm...I'm shaking, u know that? Are u stroking that beautiful cock? Wish u were here...

An agonized groan escaped him. The very thought of being inside her velvet heat had his cock throbbing. He was going to combust where he sat.

BookNerd: Me too, baby. Soon. I'm stroking in between talking to you. To be a little too honest, you have me ramped up so high, I'm taking it slow or I'll come without you.

MadHatter3000: Let it go. Come with me, Gray...

Grayson froze, blinking at the screen. His heart hammered and his mind raced. She'd called him Gray. It was a nickname he'd had since he was a kid. Maddie had never called him Grayson. She'd always called him Gray. His mind spun in panic. Had she figured it out? Did she know it was him? That he wasn't some random stranger? Oh, he wasn't exactly lying to her. He just wasn't telling her the whole truth. But he knew damn well she wouldn't see it that way.

Fuck...

Dejection hanging on him, he swallowed past the lump

of fear stuck in his throat and waited for the berating he knew damn well he deserved. Waited for the moment when she'd announce she was canceling their date and her name would blip off his screen. Except as he stared at her name along the bottom of the message box, heart hammering in his throat, seconds ticked out to a full minute, and the reply never came.

His mind spun off in another direction. An erotic direction that drew up luscious images of her. *I'll be damned.* He sank back into the sofa cushions as the idea washed over him, swirling around him like a lure. She was over there, with her fingers buried in her hot little pussy…fantasizing about him. Not some random stranger, but *him*.

Shit. The very thought had pleasure shooting to his toes. His thighs were shaking now and heat prickled along his skin. He gave in to the overwhelming need this time and fisted his cock, stroking hard and fast. Luxuriating in the incredible pleasure and relishing the fantasy the moment provided, he dropped his head back against the sofa and closed his eyes. His mind filled with erotic memories. Of her. The erratic huff of her breathing as she stroked her pussy. The little gasps and moans she made when she was on the verge of orgasm.

The image shifted and changed, and she was beneath him now, her soft body curled around his. The fantasy was so real he swore her velvet heat wrapped around his cock as he pumped into her. She'd clutch his back, wrap those long legs around his hips and arch against him.

His mind filled with the high-pitched cry she'd let out

that long ago night, and in less than a dozen strokes he was erupting. A long, low groan ripped out of him, and jets of warm come splashed his chest and his quivering belly. He continued to stroke, riding the wave until the last tremor finally faded.

He collapsed back into the sofa cushions, his breathing ragged, chest heaving. Too stunned to move, he could only stare at the dark shape of the television across the room, trying to slow his breathing. Jesus Christ. She never ceased to amaze him. That had to be the best orgasm he'd had on his own in a long damn time. Despite that she thought him to be another man, in the heat of the moment, at her most vulnerable, it was *his* name she'd called out.

His chest swelled in triumph, filled with an unparalleled joy. That had to be a good sign. It meant she hadn't forgotten him, that she still thought about him. It gave him hope. Maybe one day soon, she'd be his.

The ping of an incoming message sounded, and he opened his heavy-lidded eyes.

MadHatter3000: OMG. I just read my last message. I can't believe I called you that. I'm so sorry!

He wasn't.... Not that he could tell her that. He got up and moved into the kitchen for a towel, wiped his hands and cleaned his stomach, then returned to the couch. He set his fingers on the keyboard, attempting to soothe her. He wasn't upset. Neither should she be.

BookNerd: It's okay. We're still getting to know each other, and we're both trying to get over someone. Happens to the best of us.

MadHatter3000: Have you ever done that?

BookNerd: Sadly, yes. In the middle of a good groove, I called a new partner my ex-girlfriend's name.

MadHatter3000: I'm sorry. Was she mad?

BookNerd: Very. I never saw her again.

That, at least, was true. One of the rare times he'd forced himself to get out, to try and find someone to replace *her*. To move on with his damn life. He'd met Paige at the gym, of all places. She had a rockin' body and a sweet, upbeat nature. She made him laugh, but the relationship hadn't worked. She wasn't Maddie.

MadHatter3000: I swear I wasn't thinking about him. I was staring at you, and it just popped out.

Now *that* revelation scared the hell out of him. Had she seen something she recognized, even if she wasn't aware of it?

BookNerd: Really. It's okay. I can't exactly get mad at you for something I've done myself. So, relax, babe. We'll get used to this. Tell me something, though…was it good?

Okay, so this was a selfish question, but one he had to ask. It would tell him how close or how far he was.

MadHatter3000: Best orgasm I've had solo in a long time. You gave me multiples. ;)

A stupid, self-satisfied grin plastered itself across his face. He had to admit it. He loved pleasuring her. To know he'd done his job, while he couldn't even see or talk to her, filled his chest to bursting.

BookNerd. I'm glad. Same here. I'm fairly certain I'M the one who saw stars. ;)

He sat staring at the screen for a moment. What the hell did he say now? Oh, he knew what he wanted to say. He wanted to invite himself to her place or go get her and bring her here, to his. He wanted to curl around her, but that he couldn't caught in his chest as being all kinds of wrong. Any intimacy she granted him, he treasured. It was a gift simply to be able to share it with her. But this was the part where he had to go to bed alone, without her.

He couldn't risk telling her who he was yet, though. He needed her to get to know him first. This was his chance to earn her trust. So that maybe, just maybe, when she finally did discover the truth, when they were face to face at the auction, he could convince her to listen. To give him a chance.

It still hit him as wrong, though, to be going to bed without her, and dejection hung heavy in his chest. So, he stared at the computer screen. He ought to say something, anything, to ease the moment, but all he could do was wait, heart on his damn sleeve.

She was the first one to speak.

MadHatter3000: I should go. It's late, and I need to get up early tomorrow. Thanks for tonight. I'm glad I let Christina set us up.

BookNerd: Ditto. Can I "see" you again?

Thirty seconds passed before her reply came back. He held his breath and crossed his fingers. This was make it or break it time. He'd either gained what he'd hoped—a little of her trust—or she'd make an excuse as to why she was going to be too busy.

MadHatter3000: I'd like that.

Grayson pumped his fists in the air. Hell, he couldn't help himself. He might have whooped if it wasn't so late, but the lake around him was quiet. He wasn't sure his neighbors would appreciate the noise at ten o'clock at night. After all, wasn't that why you bought a houseboat on Lake Union? For the peace and tranquility? It was one of the biggest reasons he'd bought the two-story house. Because simply standing on his dock looking out over the waters could ease the stress of the day.

That she'd said yes, though, was a damn good sign. Mission accomplished. Now for the next step. He had another hint to send her.

BookNerd: Tomorrow? Same time, say, around 8-ish?

MadHatter3000: Tomorrow. 8 is good. Night, Dave.

Those words took the wind out of his sails. There was that damn name again. His chest constricted, but the longer he stared at the name, the more determination swelled inside of him, a locomotive pushing him forward. By this time next Saturday night, she'd know it was him. She'd say *his* name again, damn it.

BookNerd: Night, Maddie.

Chapter Six

Maddie stopped several feet inside the entrance, Hannah and Cade beside her. The small square room spanned out in front of her, a sea of people. Heart fluttering like a humming-bird's wings in her throat, all she could do for a moment was stare and try to remember to breathe. Like the last two years she'd attended, the auction was held in one of the ballrooms of a local five-star hotel. The space was beautifully decorated, in a muted but elegant style. Everything, from the soft carpeting to the draperies lining the walls, had been done in shades of blue, lending a calm air to the space.

On the far end stood a small stage, containing a podium with a microphone, where they auctioned off the men. Hundreds of black chairs lined the floor in front, with an aisle running down the center.

People—the majority of them women—packed the space, spilling between the chairs surrounding the tiny stage and the bar off to the right. Waitresses moved through the crowd with trays of champagne flutes, and music piped through the room. A crowd of men and women gyrated to an upbeat tune on a small dance floor off to the left. The entire room pulsed with the cheerful atmosphere, every face alight with the promise of the evening.

Maddie couldn't have been more terrified. Her palms were slick with sweat and nausea swirled in her stomach. She was too aware that somewhere in all of this was her date. There were only twelve bachelors. He shouldn't be too hard to find, but five of the bachelors she spotted had brown hair. He could be any one of them.

Hannah settled a hand on her shoulder. "Take a deep breath, sweetie. It'll be fabulous. You'll see."

Maddie turned her head, two seconds from leaving and going home. "Tell me again why I'm doing this?"

Hannah gave her a reassuring smile. "Because you like him, and you need this. I'm going to give you your own advice. Smile, sweetie. You look gorgeous, and you're here to have fun."

Hannah was the epitome of calm, a state for which Maddie was grateful. Too well she recalled when Hannah had been in this exact position, standing inside the entrance, terrified of the night before her.

Cade, looking gorgeous in his fitted black tux, flashed a lopsided grin and playfully shook his head. "Christina ought to consider opening a matchmaking service, because good things happen in this space."

"You're here!"

Christina's enthusiastic squeal had Maddie turning her

head. Christina and Sebastian strode in their direction. Whereas Christina all but ran like an excited child—as much as one could in a tight pencil skirt and heels—Sebastian trailed a couple steps behind, his gait lanky and relaxed.

Face illuminated, Christina tip-tapped the rest of the way and threw her arms around Maddie. Christina hit her with such force, she knocked Maddie back a step. Maddie let out a quiet "Oof" and laughed.

Christina squeezed her tight. "I'm so glad you're here!"

Sebastian came to a halt behind Christina and tucked his hands in his pockets. A grin cocked up one side of his mouth. "It helps if you plant your feet when you see her coming."

Behind her, Cade let out a quiet laugh. Sebastian and Cade, she'd come to discover, were lifelong best friends. Where Cade was thickly muscled and broad-chested, Sebastian had a lean runner's build, with wide shoulders and long legs. He had a certain boyish charm about him, and every time she saw him, his eyes held a mischievous glint. He had such a gleam now.

Maddie rolled her eyes. "You'd think I'd be used to this by now. She's exuberant, I'll give her that."

Christina was a hugger. She often wore her heart on her sleeve and could never seem to contain her enthusiasm. It made her a darn good hostess. People adored her. It was, in large part, what made these shindigs of hers so successful. More to the point, Maddie ought to be used to always being hugged, but somehow, Christina always managed to surprise her.

Sebastian chuckled.

Christina released her, a playful admonishing frown puckering her brow, and waved a dismissive hand at the both of them.

"Oh, *pssh*. I can't help it. I'm excited." Eyes gleaming, Christina took her hands and jiggled them like an excited teenager on prom night. "Are you nervous?"

Maddie let out a quiet laugh. "I'm nauseated, actually."

"Well, you look fantastic." Christina winked. "He isn't going to know what hit him."

At the casual mention of her date, Maddie glanced around, searching the wall of people. "Where *is* my date, anyway?"

An amused, secretive gleam lit in Christina's eyes. "Oh, he's around. I'm not supposed to point him out. He says he'll come out when the time is right."

Maddie drew her brows together and pursed her lips. "So not fair."

The small clutch purse tucked under her arm vibrated, and Maddie nearly jumped out of her skin. Jesus. Her phone. She'd brought it with her, so she could text Dave when she arrived. He must have beaten her to it.

Hannah grinned. "Is that him?"

That they were having this conversation for the entire group to hear made her want to sink into the floor. Did she look as pathetic as she felt?

Her cheeks heated, but she nodded. "Probably."

She pulled her cell from her purse and brought up her Gchat app. Sure enough, Dave had sent her a message.

BookNerd: You're here. ;)

His words had the hairs on the back of her neck standing on end. He could see her, was standing somewhere staring right at her, which meant he knew her face, or at the very least what she looked like. Maddie jerked her head up, searching the ballroom around her. "Oh God."

Her heart began an erratic hammer that was half arousal and all anxiety. Her body was humming tonight. Having made the decision this was what she wanted and needed, arousal had grabbed her. The luscious promise of the night curled through every cell in her body. Every chat they'd had in the last two weeks played through her thoughts, filling her every molecule with a fine, sweet aching.

Hannah's brow furrowed in concern. "What's wrong?"

Maddie turned to the left and stood on her tiptoes, searching the crowd for anybody who might be staring at her. All her gaze found was a sea of finely dressed women. Damn it.

She jerked her gaze to Hannah, panic rising in her throat. "He can see me. How does he even know what I look like?"

"Christina, perhaps? He knows her." Hannah flashed a tight smile and shrugged helplessly. She nodded at Maddie's phone. "Ask him."

Maddie turned her gaze to her phone, her trembling fingers finding all the wrong keys on the impossibly small screen.

MadHatter3000: How do u know what I look like?

Knowing he stood somewhere waiting on her messages ought to make him easy to find. That he wasn't scattered her nerves.

BookNerd: You're with Christina, and I only see one redhead in the bunch. ;)

Her heart resumed its beat. Okay, so he had a point there, but his casual comment only filled her with more questions.

MadHatter3000: Where R U?

BookNerd: Oh, I'm around.

Maddie rolled her eyes and punched in another reply.

MadHatter3000: Tease. ;) How will I know U?

BookNerd: You'll know. Tell me, baby, are you aroused?

Maddie wanted to laugh. He had no idea.

MadHatter3000: I'm shaking.

Her palms were damp, and her mouth had gone dry too.

BookNerd: But are you wet?

This question had her stomach flip-flopping and warmth blooming inside of her. Oh, God help her, she was. Her panties were damp and had been since she'd left her apartment an hour before. The thought of that fantastic chest, up close and personal, had her clit throbbing. She yearned to taste his mouth. If all she got out of this nerve-wracking experience was a hot kiss, she'd die a happy woman.

MadHatter3000: Yes.

BookNerd: Good. You look beautiful, by the way. That dress suits you. Of course, all I want to do is hike it up around your waist and bury my cock inside you...

The very mention had desire and anticipation flaring inside of her, from the tips of her breasts to the soles of her feet. Heat prickled along her skin. The shaking in her hands, though, had spread to every limb. Maddie was sure even her knees were knocking together.

She took a deep breath, drawing her inner vixen around her. She'd had one of those once. *You can do this. You want this, remember?* She held tight to the need, ignored the panic his words set off, and typed in a playful response.

MadHatter3000: Not fair that u can c me, but I can't c you. Come out.

BookNerd: Soon, baby. Very soon.

Maddie locked her screen and returned her phone to her purse, then met Christina's gaze. "I need alcohol for this, or I'm going to come out of my skin. I'm going to go nab a glass of wine."

Hannah touched her arm. "Text me if you need me, okay?"

Maddie smiled and nodded. "Thank you."

Christina stepped forward, wrapping her in another hug, softer this time. "You can totally do this, sweetie."

"That's what I'm holding on to." Maddie hugged her back then released her. "I'll find you guys in a few minutes."

She pivoted and made her way to the bar on the right, sliding a little unceremoniously onto a stool with a quiet, exhausted huff. "Red wine, please. Whatever you have."

The blond hunk behind the bar, like all the bachelors, had muscles on top of muscles. He flashed a polite smile, but his blue eyes held a flirtatious gleam. "Cabernet Sauvignon?"

Maddie nodded. "Perfect."

"Hello, Maddie."

The familiarity of the low, masculine voice behind her shivered all the way down her spine. The effect of that voice settled low in her belly and drew up flashes of memory. His voice along the phone line as he murmured naughty things to her. Her on her bed in the dark, fingers buried inside herself. God, he'd brought her to amazing orgasms so many times she'd lost count. Just the deep bass of his voice had her melting over her stool, and launched her heart into her throat.

Grayson.

* * *

Grayson tucked his hands in his pockets in an attempt to cool his jets. Every nerve ending was lit up like a bonfire and all sensation seemed to pool in his aching cock. God, she was beautiful. Simply to be in the same room with Maddie had a mixture of arousal and anxiety pulsing through him. This was the moment of truth, when he'd find out how she'd receive him. He'd either pull this off or blow it sky high.

The bartender set her wine on the counter in front of her, and Maddie lifted the glass to take a sip. She didn't so much as glance in Grayson's direction, but he didn't miss the way the liquid in the glass rippled, a telltale sign her hands were shaking.

When she didn't say anything, he tried again. "You look beautiful, Maddie."

It wasn't what he wanted to say to her. He had so damn much he needed her to hear. The need beat behind his breastbone, hammering along to his erratic pulse. He had to take this slow. He wouldn't let her off the hook and tell her who he was until the auction began, but Christ. He ached to take her in his arms, crush her to him, and make her listen.

Maddie sat straighter on her stool. "Eat your heart out, Lockwood."

He'd rather eat her. Her little black dress fit her phenomenal curves to perfection. Made of a soft, velvety material, the dress clung to her shape, with a little scrap of black satin twisted across her hips, drawing his gaze to her slender legs. Her hair was long and loose, flowing down her back in luxurious, thick waves he ached to sift his fingers through. One look at her and every one of their recent chats filled his mind. God, how he ached to get her alone somewhere.

When he took a seat on the stool beside her, she darted a glance at him, panic flashing across her face, there and gone a breath later. He nodded at the bartender. "White wine, please. Chardonnay if you have it."

The bartender nodded. "Yes, sir."

Maddie sat so still for a moment he wasn't sure she even breathed before finally turning her head and meeting his gaze. Despite her icy stare, she had a death grip on the stem of her wineglass. "Is there something I can do for you?"

With this, he smiled. Hell, he couldn't help himself. God, how he loved her fire.

He leaned his elbow on the bar and turned his stool to face her. He was only going to say this once. If she didn't listen, he'd have to move to plan B. He hoped, though, it wouldn't come to that. "Actually, there is. I was hoping we could talk."

She stiffened and slid off her stool, picking up her wineglass. "I have nothing to say to you."

He reached out, managing to catch her free hand before she got away, stopping her retreat. He didn't imagine the shiver that ran through her, or the way she froze solid, back stiff. Her awareness of him prickled in the air around them. "Good. Because I have quite a lot I've been waiting three years to say to you."

She wrenched her hand from his grasp and spun to face him, her pale blue eyes full of an odd mixture of anxiousness and hurt that hit him like a fist to the gut. "You lied to me, Grayson. Everything I thought we had ended up being lies. God, what a fool I was. I must have been such an easy target, huh?"

She pivoted, her glorious hair swirling over her shoulder as she stormed away, marching toward the entrance.

Not willing to let the conversation go so easily, he followed her out into the hallway, stopping outside the entrance. He wanted, needed, to play it cool, keep her guessing, but the words left his mouth on a desperate desire to get her attention, to stop her from walking away again. He had one chance at this. He couldn't screw it up.

"Did it ever occur to you that you weren't the only one who had something at stake? That you weren't the only one who was scared?" He called to her retreating back, then dragged his shaking fingers through his hair. In frustration. In outright fear. Christ, that had to be the most vulnerable thing he'd ever said to her. Now he could only wait and hope the words would hit their intended target—her heart.

Halfway down the hallway she came to a dead halt, but didn't turn around. He counted five heartbeats before she pivoted to face him. The tears glistening in her eyes cut him to the quick.

She swiped angry fingers under her eyes and glared at him. "That's awful rich coming from the man who lied about who he was. I'm sure you had your reasons for that little charade you pulled three years ago, but I should've been the one you shared them with. Stupid me for thinking I meant anything even remotely significant to you."

Encouraged, he shook his head, closing the space between them with slow, careful steps. He was lucky. She didn't run, but wariness widened her eyes and her back stiffened. When he came to a stop in front of her, he swore she was shaking, but she stared him dead in the eye, chin jutting at a stubborn angle.

"Trust goes both ways, Maddie. I had plans to tell you the weekend we were supposed to spend together, but someone leaked the story before I was ready. And you believed every word of it. You didn't even give me a chance to explain. You didn't bother to ask if any of that stuff was true. You just assumed and shut me out."

That article had been full of half-truths and wild accusations designed by its very nature to sell papers. He'd been all over the news that week. He'd had a hell of a lot of fallout to tame afterward, explanations to make to his employees about the real reasoning behind his actions. Most people at the very least admired his initiative. He'd played the compassionate proprietor, told them that he'd done it for the sake of his staff, which hadn't been a lie.

It had worked. People in the office treated him with more

respect and less misguided contempt. There were less rumors going around because he'd coupled his efforts with better incentives for his employees. More luxuries to show them he did indeed have their best interests and the interests of his—*their*—company at heart. Better health insurance. Profit sharing. Rewards for their hard work. Company picnics. Morale had increased, which meant profits had as well. People were happy. Everybody except one.

Maddie. All she'd seen were the lies he'd told, and he couldn't blame her.

She folded her arms and jerked her gaze off to the right. "What do you want from me?"

"I want you to hear me out."

"It's over and done with, Grayson. I have no desire to rehash it."

She turned and moved around him, but this time he let her go. He'd said his piece. For now. The rest would have to come after the auction. The shit would no doubt hit the fan when she discovered she'd been chatting with him all this time and not some stranger, but he hoped the date would stand. Maddie, in her heart of hearts, was a good woman. She stood by her word. It was a selfish card to pull on her, but she'd owe him a date, and he aimed to take advantage of that. He had things he needed to tell her. He'd bare it all, including the scars the tattoo covered and the story behind them.

From down the hall, an announcement came over the speakers in the ballroom. The auction had begun. They were calling the bachelors to the stage. He strode back inside, taking his place with the other men. Firmly in the middle, an entire hour passed before his turn came. An entire hour to gauge Maddie's reaction as she sat in the audience. Her gaze set on him. She appeared relaxed, her long legs crossed, hands folded in her lap, but hurt still played in her eyes.

The thought of which only gave him hope. It meant she still cared, and he still had a chance. Maybe it was a snowball's chance in hell, but it was a chance nonetheless. That was what he held on to as he waited for his turn.

When his turn came, he met Hannah's gaze in the audience. She sat with her husband beside Maddie. She gave a barely perceptible nod and shifted her bidding number in her lap. He smiled in gratitude. He only hoped their little charade wasn't about to cost Hannah her best friend. As he took his place beside Christina, only half listening as she introduced him, he was entirely too aware how much rode on him pulling this off.

The first time Hannah raised her number to bid, Maddie jerked her gaze to her friend. She leaned over, murmuring something, no doubt some form of, *"What are you doing?"*

His chest tightened, but he mentally crossed his fingers. This had to work.

Hannah's mouth moved, likely a reassurance, but she sat straighter and raised the number again. Bids went back and forth, but Hannah never failed, God bless her. He knew the moment the jig was up, that Maddie had figured out he was her date, when, during the fourth round of bidding, she turned to glare at *him*. When the auctioneer announced Hannah had won the bid, Maddie surged to her feet and stormed from the room. Hannah gave him a helpless shake of her head, murmured something to her husband, then launched from her seat after Maddie.

Panic clawed at his chest. This was the moment of truth, where it all either came together or fell apart.

Christina touched his shoulder, murmuring only loud enough for him to hear. "Good luck, Gray."

He nodded, stomach tight, and followed Hannah at a pace that appeared much calmer than he would have liked. He wanted to run, but all eyes were trained on him. He had to play it cool. By the time he reached the hallway Hannah and Maddie were halfway down it, standing outside the entrance to the women's restroom.

Maddie's irate voice carried down the hallway. "But with him, of all people? You know how much I loathe him."

Grayson stopped for a moment to listen. Hannah and Maddie's conversation would tell him how to play this.

Hannah gripped Maddie's hands. "No, you don't. Admit it, at least to yourself. You're miserable. You said it yourself. You can't move on because you have regrets. You have doubts about your actions that weekend. Don't you think you owe it to yourself to find out what might have happened?"

Maddie gave a small, relenting huff and folded her arms. "You could have at least warned me."

Hannah shook her head. "Would you have come tonight if you'd known?"

Maddie let out a sigh. "Probably not."

Hannah nodded. "Exactly. I hope you know I did it because I love you. I know you, Madds. This will eat away at your soul. This is your chance to find out, once and for all. Tell me you haven't thought about it."

Maddie opened her mouth to say something, but as he approached them her gaze flicked to him. Something resembling panic flitted across her face, there and carefully masked again a blink later. She drew her shoulders back and furrowed her brow, staring daggers at him.

Hannah turned, and upon catching sight of him gave him an apologetic frown.

"Sorry, Grayson. I've done everything I can. The rest is up to you." Just as suddenly, Hannah's brow furrowed, and she jabbed a stern finger at him. "But if you hurt her again, I know two men who will be only too happy to help me relieve you of your balls."

Grayson gave a sad shake of his head as he set his gaze on Maddie. "It wasn't my intention to hurt her in the first place."

Maddie jerked her gaze away, clearly shutting him out. The road to her would be a long, hard haul, but if he was lucky, his efforts would pay off. At the very least, she needed to know—to finally believe—he might have screwed up, but he hadn't intended to hurt her. He'd delayed the inevitable too long. How much he cared for her had scared the hell out of him. It still did.

Hannah let out a world-weary sigh. "Which is the only reason I agreed to this crazy concoction you and Christina cooked up."

Hannah touched Maddie's shoulder, then moved around him, her heels clicking softly on the marble floor as she made her way back into the ballroom.

Finally alone with him now, Maddie graced him with a glance. "You can go to hell. I have nothing to say to you. This makes twice now you've lied to me."

She turned and rounded the corner, pushing into the women's restroom. For a moment, he considered letting her go. He had two choices: he could wait her out and try to catch her later or he could follow her.

So, he pushed open the restroom door and strode inside. Luckily, the space was empty except for Maddie.

She stood at the sinks, leaning back, eyes closed, fingers massaging her temples. At the creak of the door opening, her eyes popped open and she turned her head. As her gaze landed on him, her brows rose. "Are you insane? This is the women's restroom."

He turned the lock on the door. "There. Now we won't be disturbed."

Her eyes widened, filling with panic, and darted from him to the now locked door beside him.

Immediately understanding her fear, he held up his hands and shook his head. "Don't look at me like that. I'd never hurt you, and you know it."

Maddie didn't answer, but instead turned her head toward the small windows lining the far wall, her voice low and impassive. "Move away from the door and let me go."

He ignored her plea and instead dared a couple of steps in her direction. "Would you have even given me the time of day if I'd told you who I was?"

Her head snapped in his direction, eyes blazing.

"You lied to me! Not once, but twice." She let out a little

huff of disbelieving laughter. "What an elaborate hoax you pulled this time, too; and what a fool I was for not seeing it. God, I thought it was so sweet when you sent me that damned book. Now I just feel like an idiot. You used all those things I shared with you in confidence three years ago against me. So, tell me, Grayson, why *should* I even give you the time of day?"

He closed the remaining distance between them, set his feet on either side of hers and leaned into her enough that their bodies touched. With her effectively trapped against the waist-high counter, he now had her undivided attention. Her breathing hitched but she held his gaze, staring in wide-eyed shock, yet didn't attempt to push him back.

"You are the most stubborn woman I've ever known. Do you have any idea how much it hurt when I realized you'd stood me up? That you had no intention of showing up? The next morning came and went and you couldn't even give me the benefit of the doubt enough to ask me if that crap they printed in the paper was true."

True to her nature, Maddie didn't back down. She hiked her chin a notch. "You lied to me, Grayson. About who you were, about your role in the company. It made me question everything about us, and I realized I couldn't trust you. I still don't, because you lied to me *again*. So just say what you need to say so we can get this over with."

"There are things I need to share with you, but I won't do it here. This isn't the right time or place for what I need to tell you." The only way to get through the thick walls she kept against him would be for him to bare it all. He'd have to show her those scars, and he had no desire to do it in this crowded hotel. "I believe you owe me a date. You have dinner with me, and I'll talk, but not here."

She glared at him and shoved hard against him. When he didn't budge, she pounded his chest with a fist. "Damn you, Grayson Lockwood. Damn you to hell. I don't care how much you paid for a date with me. I don't owe you a single thing."

Her voice wobbled, and tears welled in her eyes, cutting him every bit as deeply as the bite of his father's belt that long ago day. He loathed himself for the pain in her eyes, but he needed her to listen. None of this insanity would end until she heard him out, but Maddie was beyond stubborn, and she pushed his every last damn button. His last nerve snapped, and his irritation soared.

"All right. You want to know what happened? It took me a long damn time to even work up the courage to tell you three years ago. That night you told me about your past? It didn't fall on deaf ears. I have one of those, too, and telling you about the charade, about who I really was, meant I'd have to share my past with you. It's not pretty, and I have no desire to relive it."

Grayson ground his teeth, drawing a deep breath before continuing.

"My tattoo covers scars. The thought of telling you and having to wait for your reaction made my gut ache." He dragged a shaking hand through his hair. "Christ, Maddie, you scare the *hell* out of me."

When she didn't respond but stood, breathing hard and

staring at him in stunned silence, he gathered what was left of his nerves and set his hands on the counter behind her. The subtle movement brought him down to her level, effectively bringing their faces inches apart. Her breaths fanned his lips, harsh and every bit as erratic as the beat of his heart. All he could focus on was her eyes and the emotion ready to split his chest open, but he let his frustration fuel the words he needed to tell her.

He glared right back at her. "I was in love with you, goddamn it."

Chapter Seven

Grayson clearly waited for a reaction, as silence hung in the air, heavy between them, but all Maddie could do was stare in return and process. He loved her. Or at least, he had.

The thought made her chest ache. God, how she'd yearned to hear those words once upon a time. Now, hearing them brought up all those regrets she couldn't set aside. She'd been angry at discovering Christina and Hannah had lied to her, too, but were they right? Was Grayson? *Had* she done the right thing by not showing up that weekend? Would things have turned out differently had she gone with her heart, moved beyond what she'd seen as his betrayal, and given him the chance to explain?

When the weekend came and went and she hadn't shown, he must have left a dozen messages on her voicemail. He'd begged her to listen, sworn he hadn't meant to hurt her, that things had gone horribly wrong. He'd spoken as if convincing her meant everything. She couldn't ignore that he was still desperate for her to listen.

She'd been so hurt, had been so positive she couldn't trust him. It wasn't fair to judge Grayson by standards set by an asshole like Matt, but she was so terrified of being hurt again she'd panicked.

And then he'd stopped calling, leaving her with a hole where her heart used to be. Now, she couldn't ignore the moment staring her in the face. She had to face the possibility she'd been wrong about him all this time.

What she needed to do was to get out of there, leave this room and put as much distance between them as possible. Three years had passed. It was time to move on. Except the look in his eyes caught her. Pained accusation mixed with frustration. If she didn't know better, she'd swear she'd hurt him.

It didn't help that his nearness made her nerves scatter. Being close enough to touch him again was like somebody had sucked all the oxygen from the room. Grayson had changed. The man she'd known had been long and lanky. The man before her had filled out and then some. His shoulders were wider, his chest thicker, filling to perfection the black tux he wore. His dark brown hair was still this side of too long, but combed back, and those chocolate eyes trained on her, waiting.

Her mind filled with all those chats, with that image he'd sent her, and a flame she'd tried so hard these last three years to douse flared again, spreading warmth to every limb. It warred with the betrayal that wanted to split her chest open. These last two weeks, she'd trusted that the things he'd shared with her were the truth. She'd let her guard down, had chatted with him thinking he was somebody else. But staring at him, her breath caught in her chest and her limbs refused to move. She couldn't even think straight, at least not about anything except how much she'd missed him.

She couldn't deny it. Knowing the man she'd been chatting with all this time was him, and not some stranger, did nothing but make her clit throb. To the point she flexed her thighs to ease the unbearable ache. Being in the same room with him again had her knees shaking with the desperate need to hurl herself against him and discover if his kiss would taste as familiar as it once had. Would it even be the same?

There was too much water under this bridge, too many things left unspoken. She couldn't ignore that he'd lied to her not once but twice.

As she slowly lost herself in his eyes, the tension between them became a rope stretched beyond its limits, frayed and ready to snap at any moment.

And then it did.

Just as suddenly as he'd stilled and quieted, he gripped her face in his warm palms. His mouth came down hard on hers before she'd even managed to think about what she ought to be doing. His mouth bruised hers, his kiss fierce and desperate and tender all rolled into one luscious tangle of lips. As if he had a point to prove.

Like he poured all those things he couldn't say into the exchange. Oh, she knew that's what he was doing, because her body responded to the call of his. She wanted, needed, to push him away, but his tongue stroked the seam of her mouth. Like no time had passed at all, she wound her arms around his neck and lifted onto her toes to get more of him. One taste and she was three years in the past, pressed against his lean, solid body, clinging to him with a need she couldn't deny.

Three years spent missing him became a desperate desire to fuse with him. Every thought except the need for him not to stop flitted away, lost in the simple joy of his mouth on hers.

She'd missed this. God, how she'd missed this…the absolute desperation between them, like if they didn't stop, they'd meld together. He was warm and familiar, his scent swirling around her, wrapping her in a sense of safety that made no sense. Instead of pushing him back or slapping him, her hands fisted the lapels of his jacket and pulled him in. Her lips opened on a soft sigh, her mouth slanting over his, and his tongue swooped in, a tender, needy stroke against hers.

She wasn't the only one affected. Despite his cool, "in control" exterior, his body trembled against hers. His cock was hard against her stomach, thick and pulsing behind the zipper of his black slacks, and she ached. God, how she ached. To feel that cock slide inside of her, for him to bring the absolute pleasure his words these last two weeks had promised.

On her next breath his hands slid down her thighs. His tongue was restless in her mouth as he yanked her dress up around her waist. In one swift motion he gripped her ass and lifted her, setting her onto the cool tile of the counter behind her.

Her fingers found the button on his slacks and popped it free, then slid down the zipper, freeing his erection. As she shoved her hands in his pants, palming the length of his cock, he edged between her thighs, reached between them, and tugged the edge of her panties aside. They surged together at the same moment. Her hips rolled forward, her clit grinding against his pelvis as he buried himself to the hilt in one powerful thrust.

It wasn't a slow, tender lovemaking, the way she'd always imagined the first time with him would be. Rather, his fingers bit into the flesh of her ass as he surged up into her again and again. Her breath left her lungs on a pleasure-filled gasp, and she locked her legs around his waist, grinding hard against him, desperate for the release, for this connection to him. However wrong it might be, she needed this connection.

She leaned forward and bit down on his bottom lip, tugging on it. The action was punishment and tease. He let out a low sound somewhere between a hungry growl and a needy moan and pushed harder, deeper, faster, and the sounds of their lovemaking filled the bathroom, echoing around them. Skin connected with skin as two bodies strained to become one. His soft grunts, and her quiet moans. Anybody within earshot surely would know what was going on inside the bathroom of this expensive hotel.

Not that she could stop. Every stroke of his cock inside

her was a match strike. Every inch of her lit up like he'd set her on fire, and every hard thrust only pushed her closer to the luscious abyss. He gained a punishing rhythm that sent her rushing headlong toward total fusion.

Another hard thrust and the dam burst. Her body convulsed around him, a searing rush of pleasure that left her gasping and moaning and shaking helplessly in bliss. He groaned and captured her mouth again, swallowing her cries. His hips jerked, his body trembling against hers as he found his own release deep inside of her.

When it ended, he dropped his forehead onto her shoulder with a groan, chest heaving, his breath warm and ragged against her throat. She was attempting to catch her breath when guilt hit like a meaty fist to the gut. The trembling started in her hands, spreading through the rest of her. Four-year-old memories snapped by faster than she could stop them. Matt pinning her to the bed. The overwhelming dizziness.

She tried to drag in a calming breath, but the memory pressed to her chest like a heavy boulder. No matter how much she tried to tell herself she'd done nothing wrong, guilt and regret rose over her like a suffocating shroud. It snarled in her head, telling her she should've been able to stop Matt. That she should never have trusted him. Even now, in Grayson's arms, the terror that held her captive every time she'd tried to have sex over the last four years was present, beating behind her breastbone.

Only this time, she'd gone through with it. Grayson had made her yearn, had made her forget everything but him.

And she wasn't even sure she could trust him. Hadn't he lied to her? Again?

Desperate to be anywhere but here with the awful memories, with the sweet lure of Grayson, she pushed against his chest. "Let me go."

What she needed was to clean herself up and go find Hannah. Hannah would talk her out of the hell spiraling in her head, would talk her down from the proverbial ledge.

Except Grayson lifted his head and those dark eyes filled with tenderness, searching her face in confusion. She wanted to melt into him, to feel his arms close around her and somehow make this all better. In his arms, she'd always felt safe.

As if to torment her further, he lifted a hand, stroking her cheek. "Baby, what's wrong?"

Hot tears pricked her eyes and a sob rose in her throat, but she swallowed it down and glared at him, shoving hard this time against his chest. This was a mistake. This was a terrible mistake. She should never have let herself get caught up in him again. She should've been stronger. "I said let me go."

He backed away and held up his hands, but the awful concern didn't leave his eyes. "Okay. I'm off. Maddie, tell me what's wrong."

As she slid from the counter and adjusted her panties into place, the warmth of his come began to leak out, making her inner thighs slippery and soaking the fabric of her panties. She hadn't even considered asking him to use a condom. All she'd cared about was his cock, buried inside of her. Four years. Four years had passed since her rape, and she'd never once let her guard down, had never let herself get so caught up in a man she forgot important things like time and place, let alone condoms.

She tugged her dress in place, but refused to meet his gaze. "You need to leave before someone catches us in here together. God, what a fiasco that will cause."

She could already see the stares they'd get, hear the whispers…

Grayson darted a glance at her as he zipped his pants. "Not until you talk to me. What's going on in that head of yours?"

Her dress back in its proper place, she headed for the nearest stall. "I need to clean up."

Grayson stepped in her direction. "Maddie, whatever it is—"

She ripped open a stall door and jerked her head in his direction. "I have to pee. Or would you care to watch?"

She regretted the harsh words as soon as they left her mouth. God, she sounded like a bitch and that wasn't her, but if she gave him an inch he'd take it. If she knew him at all, he'd gather her in his arms, against that big, glorious chest, and if he did that, she'd crumble. She'd become a giant, sobbing mess and the last thing she needed was to fall apart in front of him.

He stopped halfway to her, shock flitting across his face. Just as suddenly, the expression was gone, taking the tender concern with it. The hurt flaring in his eyes clenched at her chest.

A breath later, his brow furrowed in irritation. He

dragged a hand through his hair and pivoted, pacing several steps away from her. "Fuck!"

He strode for the door and turned the lock, but paused as his hand curled around the handle then turned to glare at her.

"This isn't over, Maddie. I don't know what happened or why you're so mad. You were as much a part of this as I was, so don't even try to tell me I took advantage of you. We *will* straighten this out if I have to lock us in another room together to do it." He jabbed a pointed finger in her direction. "You might be stubborn, but you've met your match, sweetheart. I can be damned determined when I want to be. You owe me a date. Saturday. Six o'clock. No excuses."

He was gone moments later with a soft swish of the door, leaving her alone in the aftermath.

Several minutes later, she had herself cleaned up as best she could with what she had, but hadn't managed to force herself to go back inside the ballroom. Instead, she paced the hallway, trying to calm down, too many thoughts whirling in her head. Grayson's scent had embedded itself in her skin it seemed, because every time she drew a breath she smelled sex and him. It did nothing but put her right back there—the moment of total union. Clinging to his shoulders, her body straining against his. Despite her best intentions to stave it off, a heady shiver ran the length of her spine. She hadn't expected having sex with him to be so intense.

She sagged back against the wall with a sigh, regret tightening her chest. She'd flipped out on him. Over the last three years, she'd thought of all the things she'd say to him when she saw him again, but when she finally had him in her sights she'd fucked him then completely overreacted. Her words to him had been harsh and she'd treated him terribly. He was right. She'd been more than a willing participant. But her harsh words had neatly severed any ties they'd formed in those few, desperate moments of connection.

And they *had* formed a connection. He'd held her too tightly. Her body had curled against his as if it belonged there. The way he made her feel scared the living crap out of her. After college, she'd been bound and determined never to need or trust any man. No, what she'd wanted when she agreed to this date was something a whole lot simpler—sex. Carefree. Fun. Glorious. The way it used to be. She wanted *herself* back. Anything with Grayson was destined to be all kinds of complicated.

She could deny it all she wanted, but she still needed him, the way she always had.

Twenty feet or so down the hallway Hannah emerged from the ballroom, her head turning as if in search. As her gaze landed on Maddie, she pivoted and strode in her direction.

At the sight of Hannah, the waterworks rushed up on her, pricking behind her eyelids, a combination of relief and overwhelming emotions she didn't know how to begin to unravel.

Hannah furrowed her brow, eyes searching. "I just saw Grayson. He looks like he wants to rip somebody's head off. You look like you're two steps from coming apart at the seams. Are you okay? I assume it didn't go well."

"I slept with him. Fucked him. Whatever you want to call it, we did it. In the bathroom." Maddie flung a hand in the direction of the restroom entrance.

"Was it awful?"

Maddie shook her head. "Just the opposite. It was hot and hard and completely glorious. He kissed me, the bastard, then we were shoving clothing out of the way. When it ended, all I saw was that awful night in college. Waking up the next morning and all the guilt and the shame I felt…"

Hannah took her hand, squeezing her fingers. "What happened wasn't your fault, Madds. I know you know this, but it seems to me you could use a reminder." Hannah smiled suddenly and winked, although the playfulness of the sentiment didn't quite reach her eyes. "Besides. Sex in a public bathroom can be awesome. Cade and I have done it, actually."

Maddie couldn't stop her brows from rising straight up into her hairline. "You're kidding me."

Hannah flushed and glanced at the floor, nudging the carpeting with the toe of her shoe before meeting Maddie's gaze again. "You recall the first time you met Cade? He came to the shop and took me to lunch?"

She remembered. Hannah had returned with a grin so wide Maddie had instinctively known lunch had been each other.

"We didn't even use a condom, Han. The thought never even entered my mind." Edgy and restless, she pushed away from the wall, pivoted and paced the hallway. Several feet later, the emotion she'd been trying to contain crashed down around her. Her shoulders slumped as she gave in to it. Hannah was right. She had to face this. She wrapped her arms around herself. "That's the other major reason I freaked out. I didn't even think. At least, not about anything but getting close to him. He kissed me, and I just…reacted. I've never done that with anybody else. Not since the rape. It scares the crap out of me, to lose control like that."

Hannah touched her shoulder. "I know you're angry with me, and you have every right to be, but…"

"I'm not angry with you. I know you, and I know Christina. I want to be mad. I ought to be." She glanced over her shoulder at Hannah, who at least had the decency to blush. "But I can't. Your hearts were in the right place. You're right. I was miserable, because I wasn't dealing with this. I just didn't expect seeing him again to be so…"

The right words failed her. Seeing Grayson again had brought back everything she'd tried to forget. The last three years without him had been empty, and staring at him as he stood over her in the bathroom, she'd come to a stark realization. She wasn't moving on with her life because her heart still had its hopes set on him. She couldn't ignore that he'd clearly missed *her*. She loathed that he'd lied to her again, but she couldn't deny that he'd gone through a heck of a lot of trouble simply to talk to her. To spend time with her.

Because he couldn't forget her either.

She shook her head. "I always assumed when he stopped calling three years ago that he'd gotten over me and moved on with his life. To see the hurt in his eyes…"

A shiver of remembrance skittered down her spine.

"Then you need to see this through, Madds. Wherever it leads you. Love is complicated and it's messy and yeah, sometimes it hurts, but if you don't take that chance, you'll spend the rest of your life wondering."

Maddie let out a watery laugh. "Please don't tell me, 'It's better to have loved and lost than never to have loved at all.'"

"It's a cliché, I know, but it's true." Hannah laughed and slung an arm around her shoulders, giving her a squeeze and resting her head against Maddie's. "So, what are you going to do now?"

Maddie sighed. She knew exactly what she had to do. It wouldn't be easy. "I'm going to have to apologize to him."

Hannah nudged her with a shoulder. "Go find him. He's here somewhere."

Maddie adamantly shook her head. The thought of having that conversation with Grayson made her nauseated. She couldn't face him now. Her emotions were too raw, too on the surface.

"No. I need time to pull myself together. To stop shaking. God, I can still smell him. You're right. He and I need to talk, and I need to apologize for flipping out on him, but I'm going to have to explain why, and I'm not ready to do it yet. And if I find him now, he's going to do something mulish. I just don't trust myself around him tonight. Tomorrow, after I've had a good night's sleep and a healthy dose of caffeine, then I'll face him." She wrapped her arms around herself. "I think I just want to go home. Will you give my apologies to Christina?"

Hannah nodded. "Of course."

* * *

Cassie plopped unceremoniously onto the couch beside him and nudged his shoulder. "How'd it go?"

Grayson groaned and shook his head. It was half past eleven. He'd gotten home from the auction a half an hour ago and she'd called. Four hours had passed since he'd left Maddie in that hotel bathroom, and his nerves were still raw. At hearing how upset he was, Cassie had insisted on coming over.

He knew they'd have this conversation eventually, but he wasn't sure he wanted to dissect the night yet. The regret was crushing him. This hadn't gone at all the way he'd hoped or planned. "Depends on how you look at it."

Beside him, Cassie studied him, then pursed her lips. "She's pissed."

Grayson dropped his head onto the back of the couch and closed his eyes, exhausted by the topic.

"Oh, you could say that." He opened one eye and pointed a stern finger at her. "And if you say 'I told you so,' I'm kicking you out."

She laid her hand on his, where it rested on the couch beside him. "I don't take pleasure in you being hurt, Gray. Come on. Spill it. You look like someone ran over your dog. What happened?"

"I fucked her." Because calling it making love would be an insult to Maddie. He hadn't made love to her. He'd fucked her on the goddamn bathroom sink. The sad part was, he couldn't blame her for being angry, but he wasn't sorry for what he'd done.

Christ. The memories of her soft body wrapped around him refused to leave his thoughts. Her soft cry, her heat gripping him tight as she spasmed around him. The problem was he'd known for a long time now that if he ever made love to her, he'd have to take it slow or he'd end up with this exact result. One look at the panic on her face before he'd left the bathroom had given him a pretty good idea where her mind had gone. The past. Her immediate need to push him out afterward had all but confirmed it.

If he had to guess, he'd likely triggered something for her. He'd suffered flashbacks for years after he'd come to live with Arthur. Hell, hadn't she told him once that someone had hurt her? Up until their encounter in the hotel bathroom a few hours ago, he'd always assumed she'd meant her heart. Clearly he'd been wrong.

Which made fucking her in a public place the exact wrong thing to do.

Cassie let out a quiet laugh, her voice trembling as she spoke. "Gray, that's not exactly a bad thing."

He waved a hand and closed his eyes again. "Oh, it wasn't. It was fucking mind-blowing. Hot and hard and fast. Christ."

Only with Cassie could he be this open. They'd been telling each other everything since high school, since he'd met her in English class.

"So, what's the big deal?"

He blew out a heavy breath. "We did it on the damn countertop."

She bumped his shoulder again. "You stud. That's hot."

Normally, her teasing didn't bother him. This had him cringing. He didn't want to know what she thought. "In the hotel bathroom."

Cassie nudged his thigh with her hand this time. "I'll be damned. I didn't think you had it in you."

He dragged a hand through his hair and opened his eyes, surging from the couch. "Not helping, Cassandra."

"Sorry. You know me. I think sex in public is erotic as hell. I did it in the bathroom of the Il Terrazzo Ristorante once. That Italian restaurant downtown? I've also made it into the mile high club on a full flight to New York. Was hot as hell. The flight attendants didn't like it, of course, and we got a few disapproving stares, but we got a few grins, too. More to the point, having sex in a place like that just tells me you couldn't keep your hands off each other. Which means things went pretty damn well. So why the long face?"

"Because Maddie doesn't think that way. She flipped out on me afterwards and told me to get the fuck out. That wasn't the way I'd planned my first time with her to be."

"Ahh. Now we're getting somewhere. You're too much of a perfectionist, Gray, and way too hard on yourself. Sounds like something spooked her, and I'm willing to bet it's because she liked it. She *is* pissed at you, and you *did* lie to her."

Grayson shot a glare over his shoulder. "Out. If all you're going to do is tell me I told you so, kindly let yourself out. I'm very aware how much I screwed this up. I don't need you to point it out to me."

Sympathy rose in her eyes. Cassie unfolded her legs and pushed off the sofa, coming to stand in front of him. She laid a hand against the center of his chest and peered at him. "I don't think you screwed up. What I meant was, if she thinks you've lied to her twice now, then she's likely thinking exactly that…that sex was all you wanted. Now, me? I'm okay with that. I don't plan on falling in love again, and if a guy doesn't want to stick around for round two, I'll go find another stud who will. But you're not me, and you're in love with her. If you ask me, she cares enough about you that the thought of being nothing more than your next lay stung."

Despite her best intentions, her words did little to soothe the wound. He had no damn idea how to fix this. The way he'd planned it, first time he made love to Maddie was supposed to bring them closer. Instead it had done nothing but widen the chasm between them, and he'd said all the wrong damn things.

"Mmm." He turned his gaze to the front windows, staring out at the lights of the surrounding houses twinkling off the water. It was a beautiful evening—the sky dark, a few stars peeking out from between the cloud cover. The view usually soothed him. Tonight, all it did was echo how wrong it felt to be alone in his house. His heart said he ought to be with Maddie, curled around her while they slept. He ought to be able to wake her up in the morning and make love to her again before he fixed her breakfast. And staring into that inky sky, his heart filled with regrets.

Cassie hooked her arm around his waist and laid her head on his shoulder. "What you need to do is talk to her. I hope you don't plan on giving up now?"

"No. I told her she owed me a date, then I told her I'd be at her place at six on Saturday."

Cassie *tsk*ed in disapproval. "Honestly, Gray. You can be such a man sometimes."

This had him grinning. This was a long-familiar conversation. Despite her tough-as-nails exterior, Cassie was all girl. She loved pink, had an obsession with high heels, and almost always wore skirts or dresses. In fact, he couldn't remember the last time he'd seen her in a pair of jeans. To top it off, she had a romantic heart. Her favorite read was a good, sappy romance novel. More than a few times over the years, she'd accused him of beating his chest like a caveman.

He glanced over at her. "And this is a bad thing how?"

Cassie rolled her eyes. "You can't beat her over the head and drag her off to your cave. Women like to be wooed. Spend time earning her trust. You were doing fine before the auction. Go over there tonight and for God's sake, talk to her. From the heart. Tell her what you're not telling me."

"That's what Saturday's date is going to be all about." He released a heavy breath. "I'm going to have to tell her everything, Cass. I'm going to have to show her those scars."

She was silent for a moment. Cassie knew the whole ugly story because he'd told her. He'd shown her the scars as well. To have to do the same thing with Maddie made him sick to his stomach.

"I know. And I know how you feel about them, but they don't make you who you are. If she's worth her salt, it won't matter to her. But if you want her to get vulnerable, you're going to have to go there with her. Which means showing her what I see." She moved around behind him, laid her hands against his back, and pushed, steering him toward the front door. "But don't wait. Saturday is an entire week away. Way too much time for her to gather her defenses. Go over there tonight."

He shook his head and planted his feet halfway to the door. "It's eleven o'clock at night."

"So wake her up if you have to." She peered around his shoulder, one dark brow arched in challenge. "Do you know what it tells a woman when you show up on her doorstep at eleven o'clock at night?"

Grayson let out a sardonic laugh. "That I'm desperate?"

"Exactly. It tells her you can't stop thinking about her. That you have to be near her. Now. To the point that you run over there long past a decent hour. If things went that badly, then it's especially important tonight." She resumed her trek, pushing hard against his back and forcing him to walk or fall flat on his face. When they reached the small hallway that made up his foyer she released him, then moved around him and opened the door. "Go. Now. Heart on your sleeve. Women love that sort of thing. I know where you keep the spare key. I'll lock up when I leave."

He turned sideways and cocked a brow at her. "You don't. Love that sort of thing, I mean."

She let out a heavy sigh and waved a hand at him. "Actually, Gray, I'm a total sucker for it. Tyler had a penchant for doing stuff like that." She rolled her eyes, but melancholy rose over her. "Lord, I fell hard for him, and I'll never be able to tell him."

This he couldn't resist.

He grinned. "So the ice queen does have a heart."

He knew she did, but teasing her about her kick-ass attitude usually lifted her spirits. Cassie's soft side was what made her a good friend. It was how they'd originally met: He'd been the smart kid, a total geek and the new kid in school everybody whispered about, and Cassie had befriended him in spite of it. His first day, she'd taken the seat next to him and introduced herself. So while Cassie liked to play like she didn't care, the truth was, she had a big heart. She was that person who often gave too much. She didn't give her heart out often, because when she did, she gave all of it. The one guy to get past her defenses had died in combat in Afghanistan a year ago. Every day since, she'd hardened her heart.

Cassie glared at him, but her voice shook with restrained laughter. "Will you get out? Go. Now. Throw your miserable self on her mercy."

He opened his mouth to argue, but stubborn, willful woman that she was, she planted her hands against his chest, pushed him out onto the deck, and closed the door in his face. Seconds later, her final word came in the soft *thunk* as the deadbolt slid home.

Grayson could only chuckle and shake his head. She'd better be right about this, because he was about to go make a fool of himself.

Chapter Eight

"Yeah, yeah, I'm coming." Maddie grumbled half to herself as she shuffled her way to the front door. It was a little past eleven. She'd been lying in bed staring at the darkened ceiling, too many thoughts running a loop in her head, when the doorbell intruded.

She was *trying* not to think about Grayson. *Trying* to leave tomorrow until she *had* to face it. At the very least, she owed him an apology. The hurt in his eyes had been palpable, and her conscience wouldn't let her rest until she saw him.

She wasn't getting very far in the sleep department despite knowing she had to be up by five tomorrow, to open the shop at seven. While waiting for her eyes to grow heavy, she'd talked herself out of going to see him at least a dozen times. Which meant she wasn't in the mood for visitors now.

The doorbell rang for the second time as she came to a stop in front of the door.

"Okay, okay." She grumbled again as she turned the deadbolt, but when she pulled the door open her feet froze in their spot on the linoleum flooring.

Grayson stood in the hallway, arms folded across his chest. He'd been staring at the floor but now lifted his head. His gaze settled on hers, and tension spiked in the air, all but crackling. With wants and needs. With things each of them needed to say.

She hadn't anticipated seeing him until sometime tomorrow night. After J.J. took over the evening shift, Maddie had plans to send him a message on Gchat in the hopes that they could meet and talk.

All she could do now was stare and take in his lusciousness standing in her doorway. Because that's what sex did. It made her notice all those things she didn't want to see. Grayson was in damn good shape. He had the looks of one of those hot guys at the gym, with the bulging muscles in all the right places. His gray T-shirt hugged his chest and shoulders but skimmed his abdomen, hinting at the defined muscle that lurked beneath. The perfect fit of his dark blue jeans just made her drool.

She ran a shaky hand over her hair. What a sight she must make. Here she was in a tank without a bra, baggy pajama bottoms and no makeup. It didn't help that his gaze flicked over her, taking *her* in. Nor did it help that her nipples tightened beneath the thin material of her top. And he noticed, all right—halfway up her body, his gaze halted. Heat filled his eyes, and his nostrils flared, his awareness of her so keen it sparked in the air.

She folded her arms in a vain attempt to hide her breasts,

but she was pretty sure all she'd done was push them out for his viewing pleasure. Which did nothing but make her nipples tighten further. Feeling naked before him—and every bit as vulnerable—she furrowed her brow in confusion and shook her head. "What're you doing here?"

He dropped his arms to his sides. "You never returned to the ballroom. Christina later confirmed you'd left early. I came to see if you were all right."

The very fact that he'd hunted her down started her limbs trembling. That he'd come hinted he actually cared. So, too, did the anxiety filling his eyes. Was he nervous?

She averted her gaze, studying her bare toes. A much safer alternative at the moment, lest she do something stupid like invite him inside and plaster herself all over him. Again. "I'm fine, thanks for asking."

"Can I come in?"

She shook her head, peeking up at him. Him being in her apartment after what had happened tonight was dangerous at best. "I don't think that's a good idea. It's been a long night, and I'm tired."

He nodded, uncertainty flitting across his features, and turned his head, seeming to stare down the quiet corridor outside her apartment. Silence stretched out, long and uncomfortable, before Grayson met her gaze again. She didn't know what to do with herself, so she said nothing.

He drew a deep breath and released it. "Look. I realize you're pissed at me. I'm not exactly handling this right. But I need to tell you something, and after the way things ended tonight, I've decided telling you can't wait anymore."

Damn it. He'd come for the exact reason she would've contacted him tomorrow.

She dropped her arms with a heavy sigh. "I can't do this with you, Grayson. Not tonight."

She didn't trust herself, and her flashback earlier had taken it out of her.

Stubborn man that he was, he stepped over the threshold. At barely five foot six, she only came up to the tops of his shoulders, and he seemed huge, towering over her. He hooked his fingers beneath her chin, lifting her gaze to his. "You wanted to know why I didn't tell you about myself three years ago when I had the chance. That requires me to share some very personal things. I probably should have told you a long time ago, but I'd rather not do it while standing in the hallway."

The simple touch was one too many. Two weeks ago, she couldn't imagine herself having sex at all. Only three hours ago, she'd flipped out at having done exactly that. While some part of her understood she was an adult, free to do what she wanted, the memories of her rape and the absolute vulnerability they brought with them refused to leave her. She'd sworn once that she was finally putting it behind her, but all tonight had done was prove that she clearly hadn't.

The worst part was, she couldn't regret being with him. In the span of five minutes, he'd helped her accomplish what she'd failed to do on her own: take her sexuality back. Separate it from her rape. He'd made her forget. Because she felt safe with him.

Hannah was right. This was a conversation they needed

to have if she was to ever fully leave their relationship in the past. She owed him that much. With a relenting sigh, she stepped back, pulled her door open wider, and made a sweeping motion in the air.

He smiled. As she closed the door behind him he turned to her, once again invading her space and sucking all the oxygen from the room.

"Thank you." He touched her cheek, then turned and moved into the apartment, heading toward the living room.

Upon reaching the couch, he stopped and turned, looking back at her. He smiled—that tender smile that never ceased to make every bone melt—and crooked a finger at her. Like a lost puppy, she went. Eagerly. Happily. Despite nerves swirling in her stomach, her girly parts began an eager, anticipatory throb. The thought made her want to laugh. Three months ago, she'd have sworn never to find herself in this position, and here she was, panties damp, clit aching, running to him like a lovesick fool.

Thankfully, when she came to a stop in front of him, he didn't touch her. She folded her arms, her only defense at this point and a meager one at that, and decided to grab the moment by its ears. "I owe you an apology."

"Want to tell me what happened?" He stroked his fingers along her cheek.

Grayson had smooth, warm hands, and her mind filled with thoughts of those hands stroking her body. Despite her best effort not to react, her breath *whoosh*ed from her lungs and a heady shiver rocketed down her spine. She squared her shoulders.

"Old ghosts." She wrapped her arms around herself and dropped her gaze to the floor. She'd told him bits and parts before, but never the full story. Every nerve ending seemed to be shaking with an ultra sense of vulnerability.

"Someone hurt you. Back in college. You told me something like that once, but I never put two and two together. I assumed you meant he broke your heart, but that wasn't it, was it?"

His voice was low, a bare murmur between them, soothing somehow in its softness. Somehow it gave her the strength she lacked right then and the courage to continue.

"No. I was raped. I went to a party with someone I considered a friend. He got me drunk and…" The rest of the words caught in her throat. She drew a shaky breath, turned her gaze to the inky sky outside and tried again. "I don't have a full memory of what happened. It's all one great big blur. I passed out in someone's room. I have a vague recollection of someone climbing on top of me and holding me down…"

Once the whole story was out, all Maddie could do was wait for Grayson's reaction, gut tied in knots. When he didn't say anything, she forced herself to look up. He stood stock-still, staring over her head, eyes glazed, jaw tense, shoulders stiff. As if sensing her glance, his eyes flicked in her direction. His fingers immediately unclenched and some of the tension left his body.

"I'm sorry. It just makes me really angry to know someone did that to you, and I didn't think you needed to hear what was on my mind just then." Compassion and sorrow filled his eyes as he reached out, cupping her chin in his warm palm. He stared for a long moment, stroking his thumbs over her cheeks. "I hate the thought of somebody hurting you. Tell me you caught the bastard."

For a moment she could only stare at him, processing, and blinking back the tears that refused to stop filling her eyes. Three years ago, she'd purposely glossed over the details, terrified of how he'd react. To know it made him so angry he had to collect himself. To see his reaction on his face and written in his stance. For her. He couldn't know the gift he'd given her right then, and she didn't have the words to tell him.

"He was sentenced to eight years but got out early for *good behavior*." She rolled her eyes.

"I'm sorry I brought all that up for you. That wasn't where I'd always envisioned making love to you for the first time. I had lofty plans of taking it slow. Kissing and stroking every inch of you." He smiled suddenly, warm yet melancholic and remorseful. "Being near you shorts out my brain. One touch of your soft mouth, and all I could see was the desperate need to fuse with you."

His fingers caressed her chin this time, his gaze following as he swept his thumb across her lower lip. The familiarity with which he touched her made her body hum and filled her with an unquenchable need. Letting him into her apartment had been such a bad idea. She couldn't resist him like this. Sweet and thoughtful. Being everything she desperately needed. Exactly the way he had been three years ago.

Maddie took a step back, fighting the near overwhelming

desire to hurl herself into his arms. Distance. She needed distance and lots of it.

"Please don't make this more difficult than it has to be. I let you in because I said some things I shouldn't have. They were mean spirited and uncalled for, and they weren't me." She shrugged halfheartedly, as if somehow her fumbling words would make up for the awful way she'd treated him. "I had a panic attack. Since the rape, I've never been able to…"

The words flitted from her grasp as memories flipped through her mind. Previous panic attacks. The few times over the last four years that she'd tried and failed to have a healthy sexual relationship with a man. She swallowed past the thick paste in her throat and tried once again to find her words.

"Afterward, it just hit me. I lost myself with you. I've never done that before, and it scared me. But it doesn't change things." She straightened her shoulders, forcing herself to hold his gaze and refusing to allow herself to give in quite so easily. "You still lied to me, Grayson. Twice."

"I know. I'm sorry. I'll probably be apologizing until the next millennium." He dropped his hand. His shoulders rounded, his arms now hanging limply at his sides, he released a breath laden with regret. "I screwed up, Maddie. I did everything wrong. I'll fully admit it. But I meant what I said earlier. You aren't the only one who's scared. The way I feel about you scares the hell out of me. There are things you need to know about me, but sharing them isn't easy."

She wrapped her arms around herself, needing something

to stop the shaking. "Tell me, then, so we can get this over with. I need to move on, Grayson, and I need you to let me."

That was a lie and the awful truth all rolled into one. Oh, she needed to move on, all right, but it wasn't what she wanted. Not by half.

Once again, he didn't do anything she hoped or expected. He followed, cupping her chin in the warmth of his palm and forcing her gaze to his.

"I'm afraid I can't do that, Maddie. Let you go, I mean. You're important to me, and all tonight did was prove that deep down somewhere, you still care, too. I have to take the chance, whether it gets me anywhere or not. I let you go last time, because I thought…" He let go of her chin and dragged a hand through his hair, helplessness rising in his eyes. "Hell, I don't know what I thought. That it was hopeless. That I'd screwed up too badly. That I couldn't blame you for walking away, because you were right. I should have told you. But you're here, when six months ago you wouldn't have given me the time of day, and I won't let you go again without a fight."

She let out a shaky laugh. "Thanks for the warning."

His gaze seared into hers. "It's not a warning, baby. Just a statement of fact."

Baby. The term of endearment had all those hot places flaring again, had her mind racing back to all those chats…

He stepped away from her and reached over his shoulder to grip his T-shirt in his fist, then whipped the garment off over his head and dropped it neatly on the arm of the couch beside him.

"What are you doing?" Maddie couldn't stop her eyes from widening. Nor could she stop the memories from rising. The chats they'd shared when she thought him to be a stranger. The picture he'd sent filled her mind. God, he was so much more glorious in person.

"Showing you." He held out his palm. "Give me your hand."

"Why?" She tucked her fists beneath her arms instead. If she had to touch him again, she'd be a goner for sure. She itched to slide her fingers into the light dusting of curls covering the center of those beefy pecs, to know the warm satin of his skin. Now that he'd unleashed her passion, it was like a floodgate had been opened. All she wanted and all she could think was being back there, in the safe shelter of his arms, getting lost in…him.

"The ink covers a scar. The tattoo artist did a fantastic job with it, because you can't even see the scar anymore, but you can feel it." He pried her right arm loose and guided her flattened palm up his chest to the corner of his shoulder. "Here."

Her fingers skimmed over a small ridge of thickened skin sitting a few inches below where the phoenix's wing curved over his shoulder. She frowned as she followed the scar upwards with her fingertips, feeling for the end and trying to judge its size. "What caused that?"

Grayson didn't respond right away. Rather, he drew a deep breath, held it, then blew it out in a rush of air. His body tensed beneath her fingers. "A belt buckle."

The tight, uneasiness of his voice made her glance at him. He stood rigid, staring out ahead of him, muscles tense, jaw clenched, heart hammering beneath her fingers. His clear anxiety only increased the sinister feeling curling through her. He was nervous. Grayson had always been cool and in control, very self-confident, so for him to be so anxious had her stomach clenching. Which then made her wonder: What on earth could create a scar like this?

She dropped her hand. She wasn't sure she wanted to know the answer, but she had to ask. "A belt buckle?"

He gave a little jerk of his head, indicting over his shoulder, but didn't look at her. "Go look around back. There's more."

She shook her head, afraid to follow his instructions. "What am I going to find, Gray?"

He closed his eyes this time and shook his head. "Just look, because I'm not turning around."

"You're ashamed." Something had happened to him. The thought made her chest clench. She'd been sure once that she hated him, but she loathed the thought of him being hurt.

"I'm sick to my stomach, actually, and if you don't go look soon, I'm going to lose my nerve and put my shirt back on."

She swallowed hard then moved behind him. The sight of his back made her gasp. Thin, silvery lines cut across his skin in a haphazard fashion. Some were double lines, as if something thick had cut deep, leaving a permanent mark. Some were short, and some crisscrossed each other. He had a group of them, though, concentrated on the back of his left shoulder, and a few curled around his ribcage. Disgusted by the thought of what could have made them, she reached out, tracing along one scar branch with the tip of her finger.

When he flinched beneath her touch, she jerked her hand back, her heart hammering in her throat. "Do they still hurt?"

He released a breath in a rush of air, as if he'd been holding it, his chest deflating. "No. I'm just not used to people touching them. I don't show them to many people."

She shook her head, her mind racing, trying to process. "Surely during sex…"

Despite the heaviness sitting over them, one corner of his mouth hitched upward. "Sweetheart, nothing I said to you during our recent chats was a lie. You're a first for me in quite a while. I tried once to forget you. I really did. Unfortunately, I didn't get too far. But to answer your question, there are ways around that. I'm rather fond of the cowgirl position."

His obvious reference to sex should have sent her mind straight into his jeans, but her need to comfort him overrode her desire. Her thoughts filled with the scars on Hannah's face. Hannah had been in an accident when she was fourteen, one that had caused the death of her parents. The scars were ugly mementoes of the night she'd lost them. It had always been difficult for Hannah to share her scars as well. Like it or not, people judged, and the telling of the tale always brought up painful memories.

She returned her gaze to his back, tracing the lines with the tip of a finger. What must these scars represent to Grayson? What ugly memory filled his mind now?

"Say something, Maddie. Please. The silence is killing me."

The vulnerability in his voice made her finally snap to. "What on earth happened to you?"

He didn't answer at first. Instead, he snatched his shirt off the couch beside him. She caught his arm, stopping him before he could put the shirt back on, and moved around in front of him. All thoughts of keeping him at a distance fled as she peered up into his face. He simply stared, heart bare in his eyes.

Her fingers tightened on his arm, squeezing in reassurance. "Please tell me."

"My father."

He didn't elaborate, but her mind took the image of those scars and put two and two together. She covered her mouth, but couldn't contain her quiet gasp. "Arthur Bradbury did this to you?"

In the two years she'd worked for Bradbury Books, she'd only met the man once, but Arthur Bradbury had seemed such a kind, sweet-hearted old man. She couldn't imagine him putting marks like this on his son...

Grayson drew another deep breath, then took her hand and turned, tugging her behind him as he moved around the couch. He sat, then stared up at her, still holding her hand.

"Sit. Please." He patted the spot beside him, then lifted his left arm in invitation. "I can't look at you when I say this, or I'll never get it out."

He didn't have to say anything. What he wanted was clear in the defenselessness shrouding him. He wanted to hold her while he talked. She stared at the crook of his arm, at the beautiful phoenix adorning his shoulder. Did she dare?

Another glance at his face and the decision made itself. Angry or not, it clearly took a lot for him to admit any of this. She understood only too well how difficult memories could weigh on you and how hard it was to have to share them with someone else.

So, she sat. He wrapped his arm tightly around her shoulders, drawing her against his side, and she allowed herself the luxury of laying her head on his shoulder. His body was warm and his scent inviting. Bliss settled over her when he rested his head on top of hers. His heart beat an erratic rhythm beneath her ear, though, tightening the sickening knot in her stomach. He was definitely nervous. He was also trembling.

She shored up her defenses and hugged him back. She'd shared her ugly past with him, sure he'd be disgusted with her once he knew the truth. Not only had he given her compassion and quiet understanding in return, he'd respected her need for space as well. He'd touched but hadn't pushed. She owed him the same understanding now.

As her hand slid around his waist, he drew in a shaky breath, some of the tension leaving his body. "Thank you."

"You offered me the same." Her words were fumbling, likely not what he needed to hear, but they were the only ones she could make herself say. Desperate to keep some sort of distance between them, she couldn't resist adding a tease. It had been so easy between them once. "It doesn't mean I like you, though."

As hoped, he let out a quiet laugh, the last of the tension

leaving his body. "No. You calling my name during an orgasm, however, does."

A fierce heat rushed into her cheeks. God, she couldn't believe she'd done that. To know now that it was him, and not some stranger, only made her embarrassment worse. How could she deny she wanted him when she'd done exactly that?

She poked his ribs with a fingertip and was rewarded when his body jumped. "Cheeky bastard."

"Stubborn woman."

Humor laced his tone, making her smile in spite of herself. Several moments passed in silence, this one more comfortable. Ease settled between them, bringing up more memories. All those nights three years ago. The teasing. The playful e-mails. The heated whispered confessions. Once upon a time, he'd been easy to talk to. He made her comfortable with him. The same feeling rose inside her now.

He drew a deep breath. "Arthur wasn't my real father. He became my legal guardian when I was about fourteen and a half. I left home at thirteen and lived on the streets for about a year. My biological father was a drunk. He was always angry about something. One day, I got tired of being talked down to and I smarted off. He went nuts. His form of punishment was his belt. He always held it by the strap end, and the buckle caught me."

Images of a boy's body curled on the floor filled her mind. A man's face twisted in rage, wildly swinging an instrument of torture that should never touch a child's skin in anger. She flinched as her mind filled with the sounds. The slap of the leather coming down hard on skin. The metal bits clanging together.

"I'm sorry that happened to you." These words too weren't nearly enough, but they were all she could force past the lump in her throat. Her heart clenched so hard tears filled her eyes, and her stomach churned. She turned her head, burying her face in his neck.

His arms tightened around her, squeezing her so tight her shoulders hurt, but his body tensed, and instinct told her the action wasn't just for her.

"I met Arthur when I was fourteen. I was begging when I met him. God, that has to be the lowest point in my life. I used to hang outside the businesses downtown because I got bigger offerings. I asked him for five bucks one day, so I could get something to eat. He refused. Instead, he took me home, and he fed me. It was more food than I'd seen in a long time. Roast beef and potatoes and these awesome little baby carrots. Even a piece of chocolate cake for dessert. While we ate, we talked. In the end, he made me an offer. He told me I could stay with him for as long as I liked, but he had rules. If I ever stole anything or did drugs, I was out. And I had to earn my keep. He officially adopted me when I was about fifteen and a half. We got my biological father to sign over his parental rights."

"I take it he didn't contest."

Grayson went silent a moment, his body once again tensing beside her.

"No." His voice came low, etched with a hint of something she couldn't quite put her finger on. Anger perhaps. Or sadness.

He drew a breath and released it. "At eighteen, Arthur took me to work with him. I did all the menial chores nobody likes to do and I was grateful for them. I got his coffee, ran out and got lunch for the meetings. In return, he taught me the business. On his deathbed, he told me he'd left the company to me, and I promised him I'd take it to the top. And I have. We profited two hundred and fifty million last year."

Despite his last statement, it wasn't pride in his voice, but a sad sort of acceptance. He went silent for a long moment. Finally, he drew another breath and continued.

"That whole charade was for Arthur. I hated what the lies spreading about me implied about his character. He'd given me my life back. I owed it to him to earn the trust of his employees. So, I set out to prove them wrong. I got a job with the company as an editorial assistant. The idea being, of course, that I'd eventually reveal myself. How the hell it worked, I have no idea, but until that newspaper story was printed, I was just another editor. People accepted me for who I said I was.

"That weekend we were supposed to spend together, I'd finally worked up the courage to tell you everything, but someone leaked the story before I could. When you didn't show that weekend, I knew you'd seen it. I honestly wasn't sure I wanted to know what you thought. About me or where I came from."

The words she knew she needed to say, that he needed to

hear, stuck in her throat. "I can't say I'm sorry for not show-ing up that weekend. I know that's harsh, and it probably makes me a bitch, but it hurt to find out who you were in the newspaper, rather than from you."

She expected anger, more of the fury he'd lashed out at her in the bathroom of the hotel earlier. But Grayson didn't as much as flinch. Instead, he kissed the top of her head.

"And I'm not sorry for the pretense this time around. I hated lying to you, but I knew it was the only way you'd ever agree to see me. So we're even."

She had to admit he was right. If she hadn't been cor-nered, forced into the moment, she'd have run from him. Again. She'd been running for three years now.

Silence hung between them, long and heavy. This was the most honest they'd been with each other in a long time. It was good and awful all rolled together. What happened now?

He turned to her then, wrapped an arm around her waist and pulled her onto his lap. "I hate knowing I've hurt you. I hope you know that."

She could only stare at him, into the deep, chocolate eyes she'd sworn once she knew like her own hands. Something passed between them then, silent and aching. Being honest with each other had shattered the walls between them, and a fine sweet tension rose in its place. It made her tremble with need, with the desire to get lost in his touch all over again.

As if in answer to her thoughts, or perhaps because he thought similar things, his cock swelled beneath her, thick-ening against her ass. The heat of his bare skin against her arm provided a heady lure. She longed to know the feel of his body pressed against her. Skin on skin. His mouth was so close his soft, warm breaths whispered over her lips, as if daring her to lean in and taste him.

She shook her head, helplessness settling over her. "What do you want, Gray?"

"You. I have always wanted you." He cupped her cheek, his thumb caressing her skin. The tenderness in his voice made her shiver all over again. "I'm asking you to give me a second chance here. I know I asked you to meet me for dinner on Saturday, but…"

She rolled her eyes. "Demanded. You demanded."

"I was mad." He rolled his eyes back at her, one corner of his mouth hitching. "You're so damn stubborn. I knew it would get your attention."

Oh, he'd gotten her attention all right. He'd gotten the attention of every molecule and fiber in her body.

She arched a brow. "But what?"

He cupped her face in both hands this time, his intense gaze set on hers, staring almost through her. "Spend next weekend with me. Give me a do-over, baby."

Her heart launched into orbit again. Panic closed around her throat. She slid off his lap, paced to the windows and stared out into the inky night, at the lights dotting the buildings. Every muscle seemed to be shaking. This was it. The entire reason she'd spent the last three years filled with regrets, with a hole in her chest. She'd always told herself if she had that weekend to do over, she'd make a different choice. Maybe it would have ended the same way, but at least she'd know. And here it was. A second chance. Was she really ready to do this?

She had to or she'd never know. Not knowing would eat away at her soul, but how would this weekend end? They'd done this before and failed. She was finally on her way to letting him go, to healing. All she'd wanted from "Dave" was a little carefree fun, to take her life back.

Knowing it was Grayson was something else. He was a heady lure. She couldn't deny anymore that she still loved him. If this weekend ended as badly as the last, she'd have to learn to live without him for a second time. All the last three years without him had proven was that she didn't know how to do that.

But she'd never know what it could have been like between them unless she tried. He'd come over tonight and shared his pain with her. She knew firsthand that wasn't easy to do, but he'd laid his heart on the line. Deep down, she couldn't deny herself this chance. She couldn't find it in her to deny him, either. Knowing she'd hurt him was another heap on the pile on her soul. Had she done this to them? Was this distance between them her fault?

Decision made, she drew a deep breath for courage and prayed she wasn't about to get her heart ripped out.

"Okay, but the entire weekend is too much. I'm not ready for that. Not yet. One night. I'll give you one night." He didn't say anything, and the silence grated on her already raw nerves. Finally, unable to stand it, she spun to face him. "Gray, say...."

The words died in her throat. Having gotten up and

crossed the room, Grayson now stood directly behind her. He towered over her, and once again she was faced with the center of that luscious, broad chest.

Following the muscles upward to his face, her gaze met his, and he flashed another of those tender smiles, melting her knees all over again. "You're a stubborn woman, you know that? If one night is all you'll give me, I'll take it. For the record, though, *if* we become intimate, it won't be unless you want it. I'm afraid what I want is something a bit more complicated than great sex."

Caught in his presence, in his closeness, in his scent swirling around her head, she could only blink at him for a few seconds. She wasn't sure if she remembered to breathe. Had she just agreed to spend the night with him? The thought sent a thrilling little shiver down her spine, settling hot and delicious between her thighs.

She shook herself out of her stunned stupor and swallowed, finding her tongue. "And what's that?"

"I want this." If at all possible, his eyes darkened more, glinting with a hunger that stole the breath from her lungs as he touched a finger to her chest, right over her heart.

Not giving her time to react, to think much past dragging in oxygen, he shifted closer, until the heat of his body infused hers, and leaned his head down. His breath was warm in her ear, blowing softly against her neck.

"I won't deny I want you, though. I can't forget the feel of you, hot and slick around me, gripping my cock when you came. The way you shook in my arms." He let out a quiet groan, and a tremor moved through him. "God, you have no idea how erotic that was for me. I want to eradicate every bad memory you have, baby. I'm a firm believer sex and intimacy go hand in hand. I don't do casual sex. Never have. There are ways to pleasure someone, to be *intimate* with someone, without sex, and I aim to show you every single one."

He had the audacity to nip at her earlobe, sending a shower of sparks flooding her body, then straightened. He pressed a soft kiss to her lips, long enough for her to melt into the warm familiarity of him. Then he turned and snatched his shirt from the couch, pulling it on as he headed for the front door.

Shirt in place, he turned to face her. "Saturday. Six o'clock. My place. I'll cook. I'll text you with the address."

She could only stare for a moment, heart thundering in her ears. His place. She'd never been to his condo before. God help her.

She swallowed past the lump of nerves caught in her throat. "Can you do that? Cook, I mean?"

"Show up and find out." He winked playfully, then disappeared out the door, closing it softly behind him.

Chapter Nine

By the time Saturday night rolled around, Maddie's nerves were shot. Standing in what essentially was Grayson's backyard, she paused to draw a breath and calm the frantic beat of her heart. As it turned out, he lived on Lake Union, in one of those neat little houseboats she'd seen the last time she and Hannah had spent the day on the lake. It was a regular neighborhood, with regular houses, except all of them were floating on docks. What would have been sidewalks between the homes were more docks. She stood now at the end of a plank of wood that connected the shore to the walkways.

She'd looked them up once. These places weren't cheap. Even the small ones were more expensive than she could ever afford. Grayson's was beautiful, though. Two stories and box-shaped; the dark brown of the wood siding and the soft glow of the lights within made the place seem warm and inviting.

She drew a deep breath, drawing her courage around her, and crossed the bridge. The deck beneath her swayed as she moved around the side of the house. He'd texted her two days ago with the address, mentioning that the front of the house faced the lake. Reaching it her nerves once again scattered, yet desire curled in her stomach. The night he texted her the address he'd admitted he looked forward to seeing her. She'd gotten brave and told him the same.

As she finally came to a stop at the front door, her knees shook. She'd made a decision on the way over. This might be the only night they'd spend together, so she was going to take Hannah's advice and go all in. If she ever wanted to move beyond her rape, she needed to do this. It would be the final step into taking herself back.

She lifted her hand to knock, but the door swung open before she got the chance, revealing Grayson in all his glory. He wore another pair of snug dark blue jeans topped with a light blue button-down shirt. It was tucked neatly at his waist, with the sleeves rolled up to reveal his thick forearms. He had one hand tucked casually in a pocket.

He smiled and hitched a shoulder. "It gets quiet around here at night. Heard you coming."

Maddie nodded but hadn't a clue what to say, and they stood for a beat, regarding each other. She'd had an entire week to mull over this night. Three years ago, she might have gone into that weekend with Grayson with a wounded heart, but one firmly seated on her sleeve. Three years might have passed, but it felt like two days. She was still lost in his intense, probing stare, and her heart was seated in his hands.

The odd part was, she felt safe with him. Oh, she was nervous for sure, and she still didn't know if this was a good idea. But like no time had passed at all, one look at his soft, familiar gaze, and that sense of safety settled around her, warm and luscious and inviting. Did he know how much of her heart he held? How much this night could cost her?

Did he know how aroused she was? Her panties were already damp. God, even her nipples strained against the confines of her lacy bra.

Lace. She'd worn lace and satin for this date. She couldn't stop remembering the softness of his mouth against her skin a week ago. Or the luxury of his arms around her. She could deny it all she wanted, but she knew damn well what she wanted from this night: him, naked beneath her.

As if he'd read her mind, Grayson shifted closer and hooked an arm around her waist, pulling her over the threshold and into his embrace. That hard body hit hers and his mouth settled over hers. He kissed her with the tender familiarity of a longtime lover, and her body melted into the connection, into his warmth and the suppleness of his lips.

When he finally released her she was breathless, every inch of her trembling.

He thumbed her bottom lip. "Hi."

"Hi." Maddie could only stare and hold on. Completely at a loss, she held up a bottle. "I brought wine."

The corners of his mouth twitched, and his eyes gleamed with amusement. "I see that. That's very thoughtful of you. Do you think it's wise, though, given everything?"

She shook her head. "No. But nothing about this night is *wise*."

He stepped away long enough to tug her inside, closed the door behind her, then pulled her close again. "I'm not going to jump on you, you know. This goes as slow or as fast as you want it to."

That broke her out of her stupor, and her restlessness finally eased. She couldn't resist a smile. To melt into the play between them came too easily with him. In the past, it had always been a form of foreplay. "You just did. Jump on me, I mean. I haven't even gotten through the door."

Heat flared in his eyes. "I can't help it. I'm happy to see you."

A shiver ran the length of her spine, and just that fast, she was melting to his whim. God help her heart in the morning. Right then, with that luscious body pressed to hers, she couldn't drum up the will to push him back. Rather, she bowed into him.

"I can tell."

Grayson had a distinct bulge in his jeans. His hands slid to her bottom, tugging her the slightest bit closer. Until every delicious ridge of his erection pressed against her stomach. He leaned down, his mouth hovering over hers. "Can you now?"

Every inch of her lit up like a roaring bonfire. Her breathing hitched. Her pulse hammered in her ears. Her limbs began to tremble as a heady dose of arousal and adrenaline fired through her, and her gaze zeroed in on his luscious mouth. "Mmm. Unless that's a banana in your pocket."

He grinned this time, an outright, full-on, ear-to-ear smile. Her breath halted completely. Grayson had a blinding smile that transformed his face. Normally cool and in control, he was downright beautiful when he grinned. Filled with irrepressible amusement, his eyes laughed at her, but in a way that had the corners of her mouth twitching.

This time, he scraped his teeth over her earlobe, reminiscent of that night in her apartment a week ago. "Oh, I assure you, baby, I'm much more pleasurable than a banana."

The sexy rumble of his voice in her ear had her breath *whoosh*ing from her lungs. Before she could think to contain them, the words left her mouth on a hoarse, needy whisper. "I want you."

It occurred to her that panic ought to be overwhelming her by now, that those memories from long ago ought to be flooding her mind. But as she stared up at him they never came. She wasn't afraid of him. With him, and only him, she knew beyond a shadow of a doubt that she was safe. And for this one night, she wanted to get lost in that, lost in every inch of him. She wanted to know the soft heat of his bare skin against hers. To feel the erratic huff of his breath in her ear as he pressed her into the mattress and pushed inside of her. To know the luxury of getting to fall asleep in his arms after making love until they couldn't walk anymore.

And the bliss of waking up beside him in the morning.

Some part of her brain insisted she call it fucking. Making love was what you did with someone you cared deeply for, and this would be one night only.

Except she couldn't deny it. She *was* in love with him. Maybe this would be the only night she'd allow herself, in lieu of that weekend three years ago. She couldn't risk losing him again. If it ended again, the way it had three years ago, it would crush her.

For this one night, though, she'd let herself get lost in him. She could deal with the regret and heartbreak tomorrow.

He caught her lower lip between his teeth, tugging gently. "Me too."

Just as suddenly as he grabbed her, he set her away from him, leaving her to stand on wobbly stilts for legs, and took her free hand. With his fingers threaded through hers, he turned and moved farther into the house, pulling her behind him.

"There's time for that later. Come on." Moving beyond the front door they emerged into the main floor, which was essentially one room. He stopped dead center then turned to her, taking the wine bottle from her hands. "Let me put this on ice, then I'll give you the tour."

He turned and headed off to her right, into the kitchen, and she followed his trek with her eyes. A large shelf, lined with books set between a couple of intricately carved bookends, separated the kitchen from the small dining room. The kitchen itself was U-shaped, and larger than her own. Dinner, she assumed, lined the top of the gas stove and the white countertops.

He'd set the table with a simplistic beauty. A wooden table with wicker chairs. Two place settings neatly opposite each other. The floral bouquet in the center gave the otherwise warm interior a splash of color.

Grayson retrieved an ice bucket from a low cabinet, and Maddie turned her head, taking in the living room. The rest of the house had the same simple décor. White walls accented by a light-colored wood. The polished wood-beam ceiling gave the place a cabin-in-the woods feel.

Even the wicker furniture, in oak frames topped with white cushions, added to the overall homey atmosphere. Opposite the couch, two glass walls allowed a spectacular view of the deck and the water beyond. Out in the distance, the sun had begun to set, streaking the clouds with blues and pinks, all reflecting on the surface of the water.

Her mind filled with thoughts of their chats. Was this where he sat? She could easily picture him, seated on the couch, his laptop beside him, thick cock in his hand. How many orgasms had he given himself in this room while chatting with her?

The thought had heat prickling along her skin. Yet the whole place gave her a sense of peace.

She called out over her shoulder to him. "It suits you."

"Mmm. It's home."

The sudden sound of his voice right behind her startled her, and she spun toward him. He met her gaze with a smile. He seemed relaxed, once again standing with one hand tucked into the pocket of his jeans. Here she was practically coming out of her skin, and he was cool and in control. The distinct bulge in his jeans, however, provided evidence to the contrary.

Maddie bit the inside of her cheek to stop a quiet groan from leaving her mouth. He'd set her off balance, inviting her here, kissing her the way he had. She ached to press herself into his arms, to push her hips against his for the overwhelming need to feel his cock against her. She knew damn well the gloriousness of him thrusting into her. He filled her to perfection, rubbing all the right places, like he'd been tailor-made for her.

She swallowed past a desert-dry throat and forced herself to focus on his eyes. "I remember you had a condo downtown. When did you move?"

Melancholy flitted across his face, and he averted his gaze.

"A couple of years ago. Not long after we broke up. Got tired of apartment living." He slipped his hand into hers. "Come on. I'll show you upstairs."

He led her to the right, around a corner and up an L-shaped staircase, then down a small hallway. He stopped at the first door on the right. As she stepped up to take a peek, he pressed against her back. "The spare bedroom."

This room's wood-paneled walls lent the space more of that cabin-in-the-woods feel. The bed looked like it hadn't been touched. "Do you get many visitors?"

"No. Not really. You'd be the first, actually." His warm breath beside her ear startled her, but his lips moving against her skin and the husky tone of his voice gained her body's full attention. "If you stay tonight, though, you won't be sleeping in here."

A hot little shiver rocketed down her spine. Her clit pulsed to life as her mind filled with images of him, of them.

His body pinning her to the mattress. His hips thrusting into her…The thought sent a riotous mass of emotion swirling through her. Anxiety mixed with a heady dose of arousal. Would the panic come this time too? Or had things changed between them enough that she could simply get lost in him?

Grayson tugged on her hand again, leaving her off balance as he led her down the hallway. He pointed out his home office and a half bathroom, then moved through the doorway of another bedroom and stopped inside. This one was larger than the first. A huge bed took up nearly the entire room, covered in a thick quilt in varying shades of brown. Another bookcase behind the bed served as the headboard and a nightstand. More books lined the shelves. The alarm clock's placement hinted that he slept on the left, and her mind filled with visions of her there with him, curled against his back.

His arms came around her waist, drawing her back against him. His nose and lips skimmed the side of her neck, leaving goose bumps in their wake. "I'd rather you sleep in here."

That he hadn't actually asked her to stay wasn't lost on her, but his hint was obvious. His husky voice sent shivers down her spine and her mind wandered, filling with images of him, of them, on that huge bed—his hot body beneath hers, her hands braced on his chest as she straddled him.

A soft, shaky exhalation left her mouth. "Is that your way of asking me to stay?"

"Mmm. I'm sorry. You're distracting. You look incredible. You smell incredible. I'm having trouble focusing." He let out a quiet groan, and his torture of her skin ceased. Instead, he rested his smooth-shaven cheek against hers. "I've missed you. A lot. Stay with me tonight."

His words to her a week ago filled her head. *"There are ways to pleasure someone, to be* intimate *with someone, without sex, and I aim to show you every single one."*

She'd missed him, too, and God, how she ached to learn everything he wanted to show her. If this happened, though, it would be on her terms. "I have rules."

He turned his head, pressing a kiss to her neck. "Does that mean you'll stay?"

Did it?

Whatever pretense of a wall she'd had against him deserted her, and she sagged back into him. She didn't have it in her to fight him anymore. "Yes."

He growled low in his throat, a sound of relief and needs too long denied. His arms tightened around her. "God, you have no idea how happy you've made me. I think I must be the luckiest man on the planet right now. I promise you won't regret it. Your rules. I have a few of my own. You go first."

She drew a deep breath. "This is only for one night. No more, no less."

"On this, I'll concede. For now. I don't want to argue with you. I just want to enjoy the time I have with you. What else?"

"I can't make you any promises, Gray."

"I'm not asking for any. Only that you give me a chance."

She wasn't sure she could do that, either. "What are your rules?"

"Mine are simpler. No sex."

This made her laugh. She darted a glance over her shoulder. "You take me up here, distract me with your wandering hands and soft kisses and tell me you want me to sleep in here, with you, but no sex?"

His eyes glinted at her, playful yet intense. "Mmm. As in intercourse. Do you remember what I said the last time we were together?"

She turned back around, peering at the room. She couldn't forget. "Yes."

"Tonight is all about you."

"Why?"

"Because I want you to learn to trust me." His voice lowered, gaining a somber edge. "And because I couldn't handle it if you woke up tomorrow looking at me the way you did the last time we made love. The panic on your face about ripped my chest open. I'm not using you. Not in the slightest. I just couldn't help myself. I can never seem to help myself with you. You're an addiction, and it's been so damn long since I held you. When I kissed you, you kissed me back, and I lost my mind."

Regret tightened in her stomach. "I'm sorry. I said some cruel things to you that night."

"Mmm. I probably deserved them, which is why I've decided on this particular rule. But I also need you to know that here, between us, you're safe. That's very important to me."

He was serious. He really did care. Tears welled in her eyes, a lump formed in her throat. For sure leaving him tomorrow would hurt, because those words went straight to her heart. "I'm always safe with you. It's why I don't trust this."

Grayson pressed his cheek to hers, his voice a low hum in her ear. "But do you trust *me*?"

"Yes." Another whispered admission she probably shouldn't have told him. It gave him too much of her. Two weeks ago, she hadn't been sure if she could. Now, she couldn't deny the truth. When his arms closed around her, something in her responded. His embrace was so…right. Letting this happen would no doubt get her heart broken at some point, but she couldn't deny feeling safe with him.

"Good. I want you to let go. For tonight, baby, I'm asking you to trust me and to let go." He didn't give her time to respond, but released her and took her hand again. "Come on. Dinner's done. You like seafood, right?"

* * *

Grayson sidled up behind Maddie, pressing against her back as he reached around her to set the last couple of dishes into the sink in front of her. They'd finished dinner and dessert ten minutes ago. Maddie had insisted on helping him clean up—what amounted to their wineglasses, the plates they'd used, and the pots and pans he'd cooked the scallops and pasta in.

To have her here was killing him. It took everything he had to control the urge to wrap himself around her and kiss her again. He wanted her body against his, her supple skin sliding against his. He wanted her as close as he could get her for as long as she'd allow.

And there she stood, in his kitchen doing his dishes. It was a damn domestic scene. She looked right there, like she belonged, and the sight of her filled his head with visions of the future. He ached to have her here on a more permanent basis, and if all went according to plan, this would be the first night of many.

Which meant he needed to cool his jets. Except she was scrubbing at that pot like her life depended on its being spotless, and watching her drove him mad. She looked incredible tonight. Her long tresses flowed down her back in soft, thick waves. Her emerald sweater floated over her curves, setting off the fiery color of her hair.

Her jeans tormented him. The skintight denim hugged her every blessed curve, and the harder she scrubbed at the frying pan, the more her ass wiggled.

Unable to contain the urge to be close to her, he set his hands on the counter on either side of her and peered around her shoulder at the sink. "You really don't have to do those. It's not many. I can do them later."

It didn't help matters that her earlier quiet, husky words echoed in his head. *I want you.* If she didn't move, he was going to shift her hair out of the way and bend his head to her neck. He ached to say to hell with his plans, take her upstairs and sink into her. It likely made him seem as if he'd invited her here just to seduce her, but damn. He could think of little else.

She shook her head, her hair swishing in his face, filling

his nostrils with the clean, feminine scent of her shampoo, her body shaking and shimmying as she scrubbed. "I don't mind. Dinner was superb. The least I can do is help you clean up."

"I'm *trying* to behave myself, baby. But if you keep wiggling that ass while you scrub I'm going to come in my jeans." That was a little too honest. He'd done a lot of that lately; been a little too honest with her. Now his body tensed, tied in tight, painfully aroused knots as he waited for her to say something. Anything.

Her hands paused beneath the water. Her awareness of him sparked in the air. "Maybe doing the dishes is a distraction. Ever think of that?"

Now this he couldn't resist. If only because he needed to hear her say the words. "A distraction for what?"

"You. I meant what I said. I want you. Badly. But I'm determined to take this slow, so I don't scare myself again. Being here with you just makes me want. You look good, you know. I don't know what you've done with yourself these last three years, but you have more muscle than I remember, and I can't stop thinking about you in my apartment with your shirt off. Or the way you kissed my neck."

Grayson stifled a groan. God, she had to say that. Her words were a tease and a blessing all rolled in one. His cock ached. Trapped in his damn jeans, it pressed painfully against his zipper.

He rested his chin on her shoulder to keep from doing everything he shouldn't. He needed to take this slow. He had one shot at this. One night. If he moved too quickly, he'd startle her again. "That was the wrong thing to say if you're trying to keep me at arm's length. Do you have any idea how sexy you look standing there? Your jeans are killing me. They caress your fantastic curves, and all I can think about is how desperately I want you out of them. So please, do me a favor and leave the damn pan, or I'm going to do everything I shouldn't."

She drew a shaky breath, a shiver moving through her that damn near undid him. "Such as?"

This time he groaned outright, and his hands moved of their own volition. Damn her honesty.

He pulled her hair off her shoulder and bent his head, skimming his nose along her neck, luxuriating in the scent that seemed to emanate from her skin. "Such as this."

She shivered again, a shaky exhalation moving through her, and pushed that tight little ass back against him, grinding against his aching cock. "And?"

He nipped at her earlobe this time as his hands worked their way beneath her sweater, sliding upwards to curve around each breast. Maddie was a luscious, perfect handful. Her breasts were high and perky, and her nipples puckered against his palms. "And this."

A soft moan vibrated out of her. The blue sponge thudded wetly into the bottom of the pot as her fingers released it. "Who said you had to hold back, Gray?"

Now this made him stop. He released her breasts and instead wrapped his arms around her. "I meant what I said. You look at me the way you did in the hotel last week, and it'll crush me. I'm trying to take this slow, because I don't want you to wake up with regrets. Your one-night rule I can handle. If it's all you'll give me, I'll take it. But I couldn't handle you waking up with regrets again."

That was the most honest thing he'd told her yet, because it came straight from the heart. It left him shaking, his heart bare in her hands. Truth was, if being with her meant he had to wait for her, he'd wait until the sun no longer rose every morning. But he needed her to want him, too, and if she didn't…well, he'd rather know now.

She froze then turned her head, twisting at the waist to peer at him. "And I meant what I said. I want you. Inside me. Now."

As if to somehow prove her point, she reached back, slid her fingers into his hair, and pulled his head down. Her mouth settled on his, her lips plying and tugging, her kiss full of urgency and need. He melted into her, drinking her in. Christ, he couldn't get enough of her.

The desperate need for air finally forced them apart. His chest heaved with his ragged breathing, and her body trembled against his. Her eyes fluttered open again, but this time, instead of the vixen from moments ago, soft vulnerability rose over her. Her voice lowered to a whisper between them.

"All right. You want the truth? I missed you, too. I've spent three years wondering if things would have been different if I'd shown up that weekend."

Her hand once again came back, this time caressing his cheek. The gentleness of her touch had his breath halting in his lungs. It had been so long since she'd touched him with such tenderness, and he closed his eyes, luxuriating in the simple sensation.

"I'll admit it. I'm scared. It's why I'm in here doing the damn dishes. I have bad memories of sex, and I freaked last time we were together, because you make me feel vulnerable, like I can't hide. I can't deny I want you, but I'm terrified the panic will come again." She held out her right hand, showing him the way her fingers trembled, then dropped them to the sink's edge. "I want to stop being afraid, Gray, and it starts with this moment. Right here."

For a long moment she said nothing, and he opened his eyes to find her watching him, her gaze searching his face.

"I can't promise you tomorrow, though. I'm sorry, but I can't. But I want this." She lifted onto her toes and brushed her lips over his, a barely there kiss. "I want *you*. Can you accept that? That this is all I can give you for now?"

He pressed a kiss to her neck. He honestly didn't know if he could settle for one night. His heart had become too invested in her, but he had to give her this one, because he couldn't let her leave tonight. Besides, she'd been honest with him, and he had to respect that. "Yeah. If time is what you need, I've got all the time the world."

Maddie unbuttoned her jeans, shoved them down along with her panties and kicked them aside. She widened her stance, then she reached back, palming his cock through his pants with trembling fingers.

She peered over her shoulder again, hair spilling down her back, eyes blazing. "I need you, Gray. Now. Because if I wait, I might just come out of my skin."

"Shit." Of all the things for her to say. Her quiet, vulnerable words went straight to his heart, leaving him shaking with need.

He claimed her mouth, kissing her hard, and fumbled in his back pocket for a condom. He hadn't carried the damn things in over two years. He hadn't anticipated needing one tonight, but he'd bought some just in case, because he couldn't help hoping. Oh, he'd laid everything on the table earlier. He had plans for her, but he'd made them unsure if she'd even go along with them. Thank God he'd thought to buy them.

Condom in hand, his fingers shook as he undid his pants and pushed them down enough to free his aching cock. This wasn't in the plan. The rules were no sex, and he'd made that rule on purpose, because he wanted to earn her trust. He wanted to make love to her, to spend hours learning every inch of her flesh, so she wouldn't have any doubt in her mind that she was safe with him.

But Christ. What man in his right mind could resist her plea? Certainly not him.

He rolled the condom into place. No sooner had he grabbed her hips then she pushed back onto him. Her soft moan as he slid all the way into her made his whole body hum. God, he wanted her to keep making that addicting sound.

She braced her hands on the sink and he wrapped an arm around her waist, laying over her back, and let himself go, thrusting into her hard and deep. He didn't have it in him at the moment to be slow or gentle. He needed her too badly, had passed the point of no return an hour ago when she'd lifted onto her toes and thrust her tongue into his mouth.

Luckily for him, she didn't seem to want slow and gentle, either. With every hard thrust he gave, she pushed back with equal force. The sounds of their lovemaking filled the room, reminiscent of the last time they'd come together. He'd sworn when he'd left her in the bathroom that night if ever he had her in his arms again, he'd take it slow. Make sure it was good for her, that she'd come away from it with no regrets.

Now, she was hot and tight, and her ecstatic moans filled his ears. Her body shook against him, and her thrusts gained a desperate jerky rhythm. As if she were as lost in the moment as he was. Determined to take her with him when he went, he slid his hand beneath her sweater, and found her right breast, circling and pinching the distended nipple. All the while he feasted on any part of her he could reach. Up her neck. Over the curve of her jaw. Her delicate earlobe.

When he had her once again trembling in his arms, he reached around with his other hand and found her slick folds. Her clit was swollen with arousal, and one caress had her crying out. As he massaged her, her head lolled forward, her back bowing, shoulders hunching, as if whatever strings had held her up had been cut. Her pussy began a rhythmic squeezing that told him she was close. So he slowed his rhythm, taking long, deep strokes, and focused his attention on her.

It only took a few circles around that hard little nub before she groaned low and deep, and began to shake in earnest. A couple of soft strokes over her pulsing clit pushed her over the edge. On a soft cry, she clamped around his cock and convulsed in his arms. Despite every intention to make this last as long as possible, her walls squeezing him proved too much. His orgasm ripped through him, a rush of searing pleasure that had him groaning along with her and emptying his soul into her.

As he collapsed against her back, breathing hard and still shaking, one thought rose above the rest. An extended moment in time where everything became crystal clear. Despite his promise, he couldn't let her go. Whatever the consequences, he was done waiting. He was going to lay his heart on the line and let the cards scatter where they may.

He crushed her to him and bent his head, burying his face in her hair. "I'm not letting you go again, Mad. Mark my words. You're mine, and I'm keeping you."

Chapter Ten

Maddie stood shaking. From leftover need. From fear. "We agreed on one night, Gray."

What she didn't have the courage to tell him was that the thought of losing him again, of trying to somehow figure out how to live the rest of her life without him, was crushing her. She'd wanted a single night with him. A chance to know what she would've learned three years ago.

She didn't know if she was ready to jump fully into him yet, though. Deep down, she couldn't deny she felt safe with him. His arms closed around her and her world righted itself. Like she could finally breathe again.

He'd been right. She'd helped him clean up after dinner as an excuse to stall. Her nerves had gotten to her, left her caught between her need for him and the fear that still lived and breathed deep in her belly: If he wanted to get intimate tonight, if he wanted sex, would she really be able to follow through? Or would the panic come again?

It wasn't until he was groaning softly in her ear as he came that it fully hit her. She'd done it. Had initiated sex, had gotten lost in him, in the need between them, and not once had she thought about her rape. All because of him. Because she trusted him. Because she felt safe with him.

She didn't have the words to tell him how grateful she was for his gentle patience, but she didn't know yet if she was ready for much more than that, either. One step at a time was about all she could handle.

His arms tightened around her, drawing her back against the full press of his body. "I know that's not what you want to hear, but you want me to be honest with you. Hell, Cassie's been telling me nothing but since this whole damn charade started."

The name had alarm skittering up her spine. Cassie was a woman's name, and whoever she was, she was clearly someone he shared intimate conversations with.

"Who's Cassie?" God, asking him that probably made her sound like a jealous girlfriend, but he'd unseated her. She was naked before him tonight, her soul laid bare, and the sudden knowledge only served to remind her how precarious their relationship really was, how much she still didn't know about him. That he had a friend he talked to—a woman no less—made her gut ache. A selfish part of her said that someone ought to be *her*.

"She's a friend. I should've introduced you a long time ago, but it never came up. I get lost in you, Maddie, until you're all I can see. Cassie's been my best friend since high school. She's family. The only family I have left at this point."

Grayson drew a breath, his thumbs stroking her belly. "I'm sorry. It was a vulnerable moment, but I meant what I said. I can't pretend you mean nothing to me. At some point, you have to make a decision. You either want me too, or you don't. Cassie told me she thinks you're running because you care too much. I'm inclined to believe she's right."

She turned her head, peering back over her shoulder at him. "If she's been your best friend for that long, shouldn't I have met her by now?"

He shook his head. "She's told me that, too—that it would likely look wrong to you. I know I've made a lot of mistakes, but the things I've shared with you have never been lies. I'm here, Maddie, and you've got all of me. Tomorrow, I'll give Cass a call and we'll figure out when she can do lunch. I'll let her tell you. I'd call her tonight, but she's not home. She has a date, and if I know her, she's busy right about now." Humor laced his tone, but he sobered a breath later. "I have something I want to show you."

Grayson took a moment to get rid of the condom, and Maddie snatched her panties off the floor. By the time she'd pulled them on, he had his jeans done up. He didn't give her time to grab her pants, but took her hand and led her upstairs. She followed, dumbstruck once again, because she had no resistance against him anymore.

When they entered his bedroom he reached for a switch on the left wall, flooding the space with light. He turned to her, eyes luminous and tender. God help her but her knees melted. "It's an exercise in trust. I need you to understand I would never purposely hurt you, and there are a lot of ways

I could do that, but you seem to respond when I touch you. So that's where I'll start. The part of you that still melts into me when I kiss you."

He stepped into her personal space, his body brushing hers. His breath whispered across her cheek, and his body heat infused hers.

"You have my promise. Tomorrow, I'll introduce you to Cass, and she'll put you out of your misery, but for tonight, I'm asking you to trust that part of you that trusts me. This isn't easy for me, either. I'm just as terrified as you are. Of all the same things." He dropped his arms to his sides, his voice lowering to a vulnerable whisper between them. "It hurt, Maddie. When you stood me up that weekend, it crushed me, and it took me a long time to get over being angry with you."

The pain etched in his voice made her look up. Dejection hung on him, rounding his shoulders. The hurt in his eyes, though, was a punch to the stomach. Tears burned behind her eyelids and regret tightened in her chest, her previous irritation and doubts flitting away as quickly as they'd come. She was getting lost in fear again.

She wrapped her arms over her stomach. "I'm sorry. I hate knowing I hurt you like that. I never meant to, as lousy an excuse as that is. I should have trusted you, but at the time I was too afraid. I was so in love with you, and reading all those things in the paper...I didn't know what to believe. Since my rape, trust has been hard. I keep expecting you to let me down again, because falling into you is so easy it terrifies me. Maybe that's not fair to you, but it's the truth." She looked up again, meeting his gaze. "What do you want me to do?"

He crossed the space between them, took her face in the warmth of his palms, and pressed a tender kiss to her lips. "Thank you. That goes a long way. It really does. And for what it's worth? The way you feel is normal. All I ask is that you talk to me. Tell me when I'm pushing you too hard. Deal?"

She nodded, tears flooding her eyes. "Deal."

He thumbed her chin, then turned and moved to a closet on the right wall, pulling open the wooden door. He reached inside, coming out with two of his ties—one red, one gray—then turned back to her. "Take everything off then lie on the bed."

She let out a nervous laugh. "Please don't make me get naked by myself."

He rolled his eyes, but one corner of his mouth quirked upward. Then he moved to the bed, laid the ties neatly on top, and turned to face her again. Intense gaze holding hers, he pulled his shirttails from the waistband of his jeans and began to undo the buttons. Garment by garment, he shed his clothing. First his shirt, then his jeans, last his underwear. Grayson, she noted, wore skintight boxer briefs. God, he looked so damn sexy in them, too. They hugged his hips and strong thighs.

He dropped everything onto the floor at his feet then stood staring at her for a moment. His cock jutted against his stomach but he didn't move, didn't approach her.

"There. Now you're not alone in your vulnerability. Your

turn. Everything off, please. Unless you'd rather *I* undress you." He grinned at this, gaze luminous and burning through her. "I'm happy to oblige."

The sight of him naked had every inch of her attention. Her whole body hummed. He was solid and toned, and the sight of his erection made her mouth water. He wasn't huge, but his cock was perfectly shaped. Long straight shaft with a wide head. She longed to drop to her knees and suck him into her mouth.

"I'd rather undress myself." Because if he touched her, she wasn't sure she'd let him go through with whatever his plan was. He intrigued the hell out of her. He seemed calm and in control, and he most definitely paid attention to how *she* felt. He might very well be naked, but he didn't touch her, didn't invade her space. Having been at the mercy of a man who wouldn't take no for an answer, that single thing gained him a measure of her respect.

Her fingers trembled as she pulled her sweater over her head. She took her sweet time, too, neatly folding it and setting it on the floor before unhooking her bra and slipping off her panties. Now as naked as he was, she looked to the ties on the bed. "What are those for?"

"One to blindfold you, one to tie you up with." Amusement laced his voice, and she jerked her head in his direction. Alarm must have shown on her face, because he held up his hands in surrender. "Relax, baby. Take a look at the bed. There's nothing in this room to tie you *to*. It's what it represents. I told you. It takes trust to do this. When I'm finished, you're more than welcome to bind me in return."

She swallowed hard. He was right, of course. Nothing in or around the bed even resembled posts. His bed had no headboard, save the long—and flat—bookshelves. She objected more to the term he'd chosen. "Tie me up? I'm not into BDSM, Gray."

"Neither am I. Have I ever hurt you? Have I ever even made you fear me?" He lifted his brows and waited.

She relaxed her shoulders with a relenting sigh. She had to give him that one. "No. I'm sorry. You're just unsettling me."

"It's okay. I know I'm asking a lot from you. I'm not into that stuff either. Blindfolded with my hands tied, I'd be at your mercy, to do with as you please. You have no idea how much that turns me on. I told you once. You don't remember?"

A whisper of a conversation flitted through her thoughts, but the memory wouldn't fully form. Instinct told her he'd mentioned it during one of their late night chats, but that she was busy at the time he'd told her. The thought of those chats had heat pooling between her thighs.

"Now what?"

He nodded at the bed. "Lie down. On your back."

She looked at him again. "And I can do this to you when I'm done?"

"Baby, I'm hoping you will." He winked.

She did as he bade—crawled up onto the bed, laid down in the center, and waited. Every limb shook. People did this voluntarily? Let someone else tie them up and have their way with them? It didn't feel good, or like fun. Her heart hammered and every limb seemed to be shaking. Her only saving grace was that she *did* trust him.

He followed, crawling on his hands and knees, then bent to brush a soft kiss across her mouth. "Relax. I promise you'll feel good by the time I'm done. Limp noodle good."

He rose up on his knees and swung a leg over her, straddling her body. Maddie inhaled sharply as a memory pushed its way into her mind. It was hazy, more of a feeling than a visual, but there all the same. Matt's large body pinning her to the bed. In the kitchen downstairs, having him so near had been different: Grayson hadn't pinned her. Like this, she couldn't move easily.

"You're shaking." Grayson stroked his fingertips along her cheek. "I'm sorry. I suppose I should have warned you about this. Are you okay?"

The gentleness in his eyes and the warm familiarity of his voice had the memory evaporating. The panic caging her chest ebbed. She nodded. "It's fine. You just startled me."

"Don't be afraid to tell me if I've pushed too far, okay?" When she nodded again, he brushed another soft kiss across her mouth then pulled back again. Sitting upright, straddling her stomach, his cock jutted before her like a luscious treat. Grayson grinned, his eyes gleaming with wicked pleasure. "I have rules."

She rolled her eyes, letting his playfulness pull her back in. "Paybacks, Gray. You just remember that. What are your rules?"

He leaned over her, braced one hand on the bed beside her head, and arched his hips, rubbing himself against her stomach. "I'm the only one who gets to touch. Since I have nothing to actually restrain you, we're going on the honor system. If you touch, I stop."

She let out a quiet laugh, trying desperately to ignore the lusciousness of him so close. "That's your punishment? You stop your *torture*?"

He seemed to take pleasure in this remark, for humor danced in his eyes and he leaned down further, pressing his body to hers. The feel of his length fully on top of her, his erection caught between them, set her heart hammering again, but as he leaned his mouth beside her ear, his scent—of soap and man—swirled around her, soothing the anxiety before it fully formed.

His hot breath teased the skin on her neck; his voice was a husky rumble. "I'm going to make you moan my name, baby. I'm going to make you beg me to let you come. Believe me, stopping *will* be punishment."

Her breathing hitched. When he sat upright again, meeting her gaze, she couldn't stifle a frustrated groan. "You are so full of yourself, you know that?"

Grayson grinned, clearly pleased with himself. "Your rapid breathing and the way your gaze continues to drop to my cock would suggest you're enjoying it." He reached behind his back, slipped his hand between her legs and eased two fingers into her. "Mmm. I'm right. You're sopping."

She gasped at the sweet invasion. Her eyes rolled back in her head as pleasure burst from the point of contact to every trembling limb.

"Arrogant, cocky bastard." She'd meant the words as a tease, but they came out on a breathless whisper.

He chuckled as he swiped his tongue over her lower lip. "Stubborn redhead."

A heated shiver ran through her, all of it pooling between her slippery thighs. That he even noticed she couldn't stop staring at his cock and she was, indeed, aroused, only made her that much wetter. He was so damn sexy like this, taking charge.

He stroked her bare belly with the tip of a finger. "Open your eyes, Maddie." When she obeyed, he furrowed his brow. "You okay?"

She nodded, her heart swelling. She wanted to kiss him for his worry. It was working. That gentleness she loved so much about him only served to remind her that she really was safe. "I'm okay."

"Good. Lift your head."

She arched a brow. "Why the blindfold?"

"It makes all the rest of your senses take over. You'll feel more."

"And what, exactly, do you plan to do to me?"

Heat flared in his gaze. "Make you see stars. Eventually."

The exact conversation he was referencing flitted through her mind. Her first orgasm with him, when she'd thought he was Dave, just a sexy stranger, had been incredible, and he hadn't even touched her. Her orgasm, when he'd fucked her on the vanity in the hotel bathroom, had left her breathless. Knowing the pleasure he could bring her had her clit begging for his touch.

She moaned and squeezed her thighs together to ease the ache he already built.

"Oh, God." She closed her eyes and did as he bade, lifting her head.

He put one of the ties over her eyes, securing the back tightly enough that she couldn't see, but didn't appear to knot it. "All right. Now your hands. Hold them up in front of you, please."

She did. This time, he tied the silk tight enough she couldn't pull her hands apart, then took her wrists and gently placed her arms over her head.

"Is this okay?" His voice came as a murmur beside her ear, his breath hot against the lobe.

She groaned, frustration and need winding through her. "No. I can't see you. I can't touch you. This is driving me crazy."

"That's the whole idea. But what I meant was, does the position hurt your arms at all?"

She sighed. "No. I'm comfortable with the position."

"Good. Now don't move. Pretend you *are* tied to the bed, that your wrists are restrained. And remember. If you touch, I'll stop, and believe me, I'll make sure you don't want me to." His mouth brushed hers, his voice a low hum between them. "I promise you'll enjoy it. Do you trust me, Maddie?"

She nodded, once again breathless. "I trust you."

"Good." He kissed her again, a tender tangle of his lips with hers, then pulled away.

His fingers caressed the tip of her right breast first, circling the nipple, his touch so light goose bumps shivered across her skin. No sooner had he touched her, though, than he retreated. He shifted, moving off her, and the bed dipped. His fingers skimmed her belly next, running down the center, then retreated. Next, he caressed his warm palms up her thighs, grazing her nether lips with his thumbs.

Maddie sucked in a sharp breath. Desire tore through her, and her hips arched off the bed. Barely a minute and already he had her panting. When he retreated again, she moaned, lifted her arms and reached out in the direction she swore he was in.

"Ah, ah, ah." His voice held a tease and, damn him, seemed to come from across the room.

She let her arms drop back over her head with a frustrated sigh. "I hate not touching you."

He chuckled and as suddenly as he seemed to disappear, he came close and his hot tongue flicked over her earlobe. "Am I driving you crazy?"

His husky rumble in her ear sent shivers down her spine that all settled between her thighs.

She rolled her head back and forth, thrusting her chin and her breasts out with the frustration winding through her. "Yes!"

"Do you remember what I said? It'll be worth it. Trust me?"

She sighed, allowing her muscles to relax. "Yes."

Time passed slowly after that. He seemed constantly on the move around her, keeping her disoriented enough she couldn't pinpoint where he'd touch next. A light caress over her nipples. A firm stroke of his palms over her belly. A fingertip skimming her ankle. Occasionally, he'd touch her in intimate places, stroking his fingers over her mound, inserting a digit inside her, but as soon as she arched into the touch and began to enjoy it, he'd take it away.

He stroked the tip of his cock across her lips once. Across the tips of her breasts. He rubbed his erection against her mound as his body hovered over hers. Every touch made her yearn, and each one stoked the fire within her, sending it racing across her skin. Not once did her bad memories invade her thoughts nor did anxiety creep over her, because he kept her focused on him, on the ache he created low in her belly. He had her panting. Every nerve ending had come alive, and her body vibrated with a need so keen she was sure she'd come the next time he touched her.

The bed dipped, his warm, soft skin pressing against her side. His hip? He confirmed the thought when he rocked his erection against her thigh. His warm palm skimmed down her belly to settle over her mound.

His long fingers rested along her slit. "How you doing?"

His voice rumbled beside her ear again, and she squirmed, her heels slipping over the sheets as she shifted her legs. She longed to press them together, to open them and arch into his hand, but once again he retreated.

She finally gave in, going still on the bed. "I ache. Please, Gray, enough. Touch me."

And then he did. His palm slid over her mound again, one long finger sliding between her lips to stroke her engorged clit. Her back arched off the bed with the pleasure that roared through her. A quiet, desperate moan escaped her.

He didn't tease this time, though. That delicious finger stroked and circled, and her orgasm slammed into her. Every muscle tightened and loosened in a white hot rush of juices, leaving her gasping and shaking and sighing. Grayson didn't stop there. He continued to stroke her sensitive clit, and one orgasm rolled into two, then three. He caressed her until she was breathless, her body taut as a bowstring with the unbelievable pleasure gripping her.

When the quaking finally subsided, he eased his fingers from her. Panting and spent, she collapsed back into the softness of the quilt. She lay there stunned and boneless.

Grayson stretched out beside her, his cock once again hot and hard against her thigh, and pressed a soft kiss to her neck, below her earlobe. "You okay?"

Maddie let out a breathless laugh. He'd made good on this threat. To come that hard and still want him amazed her, but she did. She wanted him buried deep inside of her. "I'm not sure I can move, but yeah. I am sooo good."

He laughed, turned her head toward him with one finger, and brushed a tender kiss across her mouth. Then reached over her head and pulled off the blindfold before doing the same to her wrists. He tossed both ties onto the bed beside her and stroked his fingers over her lips. "Worth it?"

Was it? Hands down, but now that she'd calmed down enough to catch her breath, his cock against her thigh became her focus. It was his turn now.

Deciding to show him rather than answer, she sat up and moved over him, rolling him onto his back. She braced her hands on his chest and settled on top of him, rubbing her slippery slit along the length of his erection. "You tell me."

He groaned, his eyes heavy-lidded and blazing, and gripped her thighs, fingers digging hard into her skin. "Is this your idea of payback? Because it's working. When you came, I damn near came with you."

He was as breathless as she was, and another slide over his length had his eyes rolling back and closing. She grinned, heart full and light. To be with him this way was gloriously freeing and as easy as breathing. Knowing she had power over him was the ultimate lure. He'd indeed made her see stars, and she intended to repay the debt.

"Your no sex rule? I'm vetoing it, because I want you. I want this cock inside me." She reached behind her, stroking as much of him as she could reach, then leaned down and caught his bottom lip between her teeth. "Condoms, Gray. Tell me you have more condoms."

He groaned again, his body beginning to shake in earnest now, and opened his eyes. "Top shelf." He went still and his features sobered. "We forgot that first time."

She stilled, remembering, and nodded. "Yeah."

His thumbs stroked her skin, his gaze searching hers anxiously. "You do know, if you end up pregnant…"

"I know, but thank you for saying it." She leaned down and brushed a kiss over his mouth. The thought of a baby was a double-edged sword. Things were so up in the air between them. They weren't quite right yet. A baby would only complicate their relationship. It hadn't occurred to her until he said the words, though, how much she needed to hear him say them. She was grateful.

She rose up on her knees, stretching to reach the top shelf. Her fingers found a rather large box, and she grinned as she pulled it down. He'd bought a twelve pack.

She glanced at him as she resettled herself on his hips and opened one end of the box. "Sure of yourself, aren't you?"

"No. Just hopeful." He winked and nodded at the box in her hands. "Condom. I'm dying here."

She couldn't resist teasing, sliding her slickness along his length again as she moved down his body. "Is this killing you?"

As hoped, his eyes fluttered closed and his jaw clenched. "And you damn well know it. Baby, I'm on my knees." His hands slid up her stomach, closing over her breasts, thumbs sweeping her nipples. "I'm probably going to embarrass myself and come as soon as you sink onto me. For the love of God, woman, have mercy. I need you. Badly."

The need in his voice had the same feeling rising within her and the desire to tease again fled as quickly as it came. His little torture routine had made her feel closer to him, and for tonight at least she wanted to relish it.

She drew out a row of condoms, ripped one off, and set the box back on the shelf. Then she leaned down, whispering against his mouth. "I need you, too."

His eyes opened. Something hot and needy moved between them in that tiny space and his arms came around her, holding her close. He lifted his head, brushing his mouth over hers. "Condom, baby."

She nodded and tore open the packet, slid the rubber down his length, then moved up and rose over him. As she took him inch by inch, he sat upright, wrapping his arms tightly around her. She was desperate—for relief, for the connection. Her body came alive all over again, fire racing along her skin. His shaking told her he was in a similar place, but she wanted this to last as long as possible. She didn't want to think of tomorrow or regrets. Only of the intimacy flowing between them.

With his gaze locked on hers, she lost herself in his eyes, and that connection rose between them. They rocked against each other, the extended movements luxurious and slow. Despite his emphatic plea to put him out of his misery, he didn't seem in any hurry. Rather, he held her tightly, taking every erratic, hot breath with her.

His cock filled her, and every inch hit the exact right spot. If she rolled her hips forward, her clit rubbed his pelvis, charging her up all over again. In minutes she was trembling from head to toe, ready to combust. Every thrust propelled her closer to the edge, and she fell into a desperate, jerky rhythm as she lost herself in the unbelievable pleasure.

She wasn't alone in that, either. Grayson's body trembled against hers, his breathing gaining an erratic huff, his eyes heavy-lidded. His hands slid down her back to her buttocks, and as she sank and ground against him, his large, warm hands yanked her to him faster and harder. They gained a frantic gait, bodies shoving together, the sound of skin slapping skin in the otherwise quiet room.

She couldn't be sure who tipped first, but mid-thrust her orgasm rushed over her, this one a flood of wetness, luxurious and bone-melting. She dropped her head back, sighing and shaking helplessly in his arms.

Grayson groaned in her ear, a desperate, relieved sound. His belly quivered against hers as he found his own release.

When the spasms released her, she lifted her head, breathless and in awe. He watched her, tenderness in his eyes. His hands stroked her body, up and down her back, over the curve of her buttocks and down her thighs. In his intense gaze, the reality of exactly where she'd ended up slammed into her. How would she ever summon the courage to let him go now?

Tears pricked at her eyes. She couldn't. Right or wrong, good or bad, her heart was invested in him. It was a moment of absolute clarity and desperate surrender all rolled into one tangle of emotion that caught in her throat and wanted to rip her chest open. She needed him, whether she wanted to or not. His strength, his gentle presence, the way he made her feel safe, truly safe, for the first time in four years—however long their relationship lasted, she'd take it, because she couldn't let him go.

Shaking and overwhelmed by the moment and the man, she wrapped her arms around him and buried her face in his throat. The tears refused to be held back anymore and leaked down her cheeks onto his shoulder as she surrendered.

Grayson stroked her back. "What's wrong?"

She snuggled deeper into him, wrapping as much of herself around him as she could. They were as close as two people could get, but she couldn't seem to get close enough. Not by half.

"Just don't let go." She murmured against his throat, letting his scent wash over her and soothe the panic gripping her chest. "Don't ever let go."

If he did, she might come apart at the seams.

Grayson crushed her to him and buried his face in her hair. "I won't let go, Maddie, I promise. Not ever again."

Chapter Eleven

Grayson woke the next morning lighter than he'd been in a while. More sated as well. Beside him, Maddie continued to sleep, her breathing deep and even. She lay on her side, her glorious hair fanning the pillow around her head. She'd also hogged the covers, pulling the majority of his king-sized quilt to her side and wrapping it around herself. Not that he could begrudge her the tiny liberty.

He lay there watching her for a good ten minutes. He liked the sight of her in his bed. Liked, too, the relaxed, peaceful look on her face, and the way she'd stayed by his side all night. Despite the fact that she had the entire rest of the bed, she'd slept curled against him. He'd fallen asleep wrapped in her arms, and had awakened to her soft, warm breaths on his face.

Somewhere over the last ten minutes, he'd made a decision: Maddie in his bed ought to be an every night occurrence. He wanted to wake up to her like this every morning.

He wanted her to be a permanent part of his world. So he'd make her one. Or at least, he had plans to try. He'd do what he wanted to three years ago, before the infamous weekend where everything blew up in his face.

He'd ask her to marry him.

They had to get through breakfast, of course, and he'd need a ring. And he wanted to do it right, though the details eluded him. He'd need Cassie's help. First, though, he needed coffee.

He pressed a soft kiss to Maddie's lips then rose from the bed, found his shorts where he'd dropped them the night before, and pulled them on before heading downstairs into the kitchen. First up was coffee. The scent of a fresh brew would no doubt wake sleepyhead upstairs.

When he was halfway through making the omelets, the telltale creak of the floorboards upstairs told him Maddie had woken. A minute later the toilet flushed and the water ran, followed by more silence. A minute later the stairs issued a groan.

"Morning."

The soft sound of her voice had a smile spreading clear across his face. His heart skipped a beat as he flipped the omelet closed and turned to look at her.

His mouth dropped open. She stood at the edge of the kitchen, her eyes soft but bright…wearing the shirt he'd discarded last night. The light blue dress shirt hung to mid-thigh, and she'd had to roll up the sleeves, but damn.

He followed the line of her body, unable to hide his surprise. "Wow. Look at you."

"Hope it's okay that I stole it." She gripped the open neck and brought it to her nose, inhaling. "It smells like you, and I didn't want to put on yesterday's clothes yet."

"Oh, believe me, I don't mind." He took a step to his left and bent to brush a kiss across her mouth. "Feel free to keep that. It looks much better on you."

Her lips melted beneath his, and she leaned into him, and what began as a simple good morning peck became hot and needy. He was turning fully toward her when she giggled and pulled away enough to meet his gaze. Her eyes gleamed. "You're burning breakfast."

He swore under his breath and slid the pan from the burner, lifting the edge of the eggs to peek at the underside. They were little overdone, but not burnt. Thank God.

He tossed her a playful glare. "See what you do to me? Make me forget myself."

"I'd say I was sorry, but I'd be lying." She sighed, an entirely too pleased smile blooming on her face, and stepped up beside him, peering around his shoulder. "Smells good. What's for breakfast?"

"Omelets. With spinach, tomatoes, and mozzarella."

"With egg whites?" She looked up at him, one brow arched in disbelief, then stared at the pan again as if she couldn't be sure she actually wanted to eat it.

He shrugged and grinned. "I like eggs for breakfast, good protein, but I don't eat very many whole eggs. Too much fat. You'll like it. Trust me." He nodded toward the coffee pot, several feet down the counter. "I made coffee. Sugar's in the bowl. Half and half is still in the fridge."

She froze then, staring wide-eyed at him for a moment. "You remembered how I like my coffee."

They used to share a lot of coffee. Their first official date back way back when had been over a cup at Starbucks. She also knew he took his black. He wasn't into what he liked to call *fancy* coffee. Give him a plain ol' cup of joe over Frappuccinos or lattes any day. He preferred his food the same way—simple.

Maddie, however, had a love affair with lattes. So when he'd gone to the grocery store yesterday to pick up the ingredients for dinner, he'd made sure to pick up sugar and half and half as well. Along with the condoms, picking up those items had been hopeful thinking, but he was glad he'd done it.

He leaned over, murmuring against her lips as he brushed another kiss across her mouth. "I remember everything."

She blinked at him again, then in a sudden flurry of movement, threw her arms around his neck and plastered her mouth to his. She didn't hold back, either, but leaned into him, her soft lips coaxing his open. By the time she pulled back again, breakfast was all but forgotten.

He settled his hands on her hips, turned her ninety degrees and lifted her, setting her onto the island countertop, then eased between her thighs.

"That was the exact wrong thing to do if you want that coffee anytime soon." He reattached his mouth to hers, stroking the seam of her lips as his hands gained a mind of their own, wandering up her smooth thighs and beneath the hem of his shirt. When he reached her bottom, a groan escaped him. "You're naked under here. Christ. Hope you weren't hungry, because I think breakfast will have to wait."

She didn't push him away either, but slid forward on the counter, settling her heat against the erection pulsing to life in his shorts.

"I'm not hungry. At least not for food. Coffee can wait. I have to leave soon. Need to be at the shop by eleven, and I still need to go home and shower." She nipped at his bottom lip, tugging gently on it. Then she reached into the breast pocket of the shirt and came out with a condom. "Can you make do with that time, Book Nerd?"

"Minx. You had every intention of sabotaging me." He shoved his underwear down, kicked them aside, and took the condom from her fingers, waggling his brows as he rolled the latex down his length. "You can shower here. I'll even help."

Condom in place, he slid his hands up her thighs to the soft, firm globes of her ass and pulled her to him. She surged with him, sliding onto him in one hard, desperate thrust, and moaned low in her throat. He groaned as pleasure slid to his toes.

Her head dropped back, her hair spilling down her back, her body already shaking. "H-hazard of waking up in your b-bed is the whole house smells like you. It made me wet."

She wasn't kidding. She was hot and slippery and every stroke sent them hurtling toward bliss as they thrust hard against each other. Despite falling asleep more sated than he ever remembered being, their coupling didn't last long. In a couple dozen strokes, they were shuddering together, the quiet kitchen filling with her cries as she shattered around him.

Minutes later, she lounged with her head against his chest. Something intense seemed to rise over her, almost a sadness. "I have to go. I wanted one more time with you before I had to leave."

Face still buried in the fall of her hair, arms around her, he couldn't bring himself to let go even enough to meet her gaze. Damn, he hated good-byes. They'd said way too many of them. Her clear upset had his chest tightening. Had she meant what she said? Was she reverting to their original deal, one night only?

It was a damn vulnerable thing to ask, but he had to know. "Can I see you tonight? I have something I need to do today, but I should be done by the time your shop closes at six. We could have dinner, maybe go see a movie."

She paused for a split second, going absolutely still, before she lifted her head to look at him. Her gaze roamed his face anxiously. "I'd like that."

The tightness in his chest eased and he leaned in to brush a kiss across her mouth. "You scared me. You were tense for a minute. Thought maybe you were trying to give me a hint."

Her cheeks flushed and she dropped her gaze to his chest. "I was thinking about something. Plus, I didn't want to assume..."

"Assume, baby. Please always assume I want more of you. As much as you'll let me have." He kissed her again, relieved when she leaned into him. He stroked the contours of her face. "What were you thinking about?"

She stared at him for a moment, eyes searching, then drew a deep breath. "I wanted to thank you."

The nervous flit of her gaze had his gut tightening. "What for, baby?"

She dropped her gaze, stroking her hands idly over his chest. "This. Us. For having patience with me. The first time we made love, in that hotel bathroom…"

He swallowed a miserable groan. That had not been making love and had not at all been his best effort. He'd be making up for that for years to come. Assuming she'd let him, anyway.

He stroked his thumbs over her thighs, where he still held on to her. "What about it?"

"I panicked that night. Because you hit a trigger for me. It was the first time since my rape in college that I'd ever been able to…" She shook her head, her throat bobbing as she swallowed. "It's always been in the back of my mind. But I was sitting here realizing that I hadn't thought about it when I came downstairs. I got lost. In you."

She shrugged halfheartedly and finally looked up at him, eyes searching his in a way that humbled him. To know someone had hurt her that way filled him with a fury he didn't know what to do with. He wanted to find the bastard and beat him senseless, but knowing he could make her forget? That she trusted him enough to let go like that? God.

"You humble me. I'm glad. We'll make more good memories. I promise." He pressed a tender kiss to her lips. "So, we're on for tonight then?"

She nodded. "Tonight."

* * *

An hour later, he stood in the private vestibule outside Cassie's upscale condo. Cassie, of course, even had expensive taste in condos. She'd bought the penthouse in one of the most premier condominium towers in Seattle. When no sound registered from within, he punched the doorbell again, four times in quick secession. Enough to be annoying. She hated when people did that, but it would make her get up to answer the door, if only so she could tell whoever it was to knock it the hell off.

Distinct grumbling finally registered from the other side of the door, and Grayson prepared himself for the crankiness about to come. And for sure she would be: it was barely ten a.m. on a Sunday morning, and Cassie almost always had a date on Saturday nights. If he was lucky, the dude wouldn't still be in her bed.

She didn't disappoint. When she yanked the door open, her face was twisted in irritation, eyes narrowed in warning.

"What." She spit the word out, but at the sight of him rolled her eyes. "Oh, it's you. What in God's name do you want so early in the morning?"

Her short hair was mussed, parts of it sticking straight out from her head, and bags underlined her normally bright eyes. She clutched the sides of her silk robe closed by folding her arms. Someone had most definitely gone out partying last night.

Grayson grinned. "Rough night?"

She glared at him. "And it just ended a few hours ago."

He peered around her, searching out any sign that her night hadn't completely ended. "You alone?"

Cassie furrowed her brow. "He left last night. What—"

"Good." He pushed past her into the apartment, striding for the living room.

"Sure, Gray, come on in." She mumbled behind him, her voice laced with exhaustion and irritation, but closed the door, calling to him as she followed him. "What on earth has you so perky this early in the morning?"

Unable to contain the giddiness trapped in his chest, he bounced on the balls of his feet as he faced her. "I need your help."

Cassie stopped in front of him, head tipped back as she peered up at him. Her gaze worked over his face for a few seconds, searching, before a knowing grin blossomed. Her tired eyes illuminated as understanding dawned in her face. "She stayed."

"All damn night."

She punched him lightly on the shoulder. "Go you. It was awesome, I take it?"

"And then some. Which is why I need your help." He stuffed his hands in his pockets, hoping she'd remember what he was about to tell her. "Do you recall a conversation we had three years ago, right before I planned that weekend? There was something I told you I'd eventually like you to do, something I needed help with. I decided to wait until after I told Maddie everything."

It was cruel to tease her, to drag this out, given how tired she was. If he knew her, she hadn't gotten much sleep the night before, but she'd been supportive of everything he'd ever done. He wanted to watch her face when she figured out his plans.

It took her a bit. She gnawed her lower lip between her teeth, her eyes narrowed. Several ticks of the clock later, her eyes flew open wide and her jaw dropped.

One hand flew to cover her mouth, her voice muffled behind her fingers. "Oh my God. You're going to ask her."

He nodded, unable to contain what surely had to be a goofy-ass grin. "Tonight. But I need a ring."

Cassie squealed and hurled herself against him, squeezing him tight. "Oh my God, Gray. I'm so damn happy for you I could just die right here. You've waited three long years for this moment. You must be beside yourself."

He hugged her back. "And nervous. I haven't a clue about picking out a ring. You were fabulous help with that bracelet. She wore it last night. Will you help?"

She leaned back, arms hooked around his waist. "Of course. Oh, I've got so many rings to show you. We've started a new line of jewelry, and I have some I think she'd love. But did it have to be at ten o'clock in the morning?" She waved a flippant hand in the air, one corner of her mouth quirking upward. "Couldn't it have waited until, oh, say, noon?"

He grimaced. "I know it's early for you, but I want to get this done as early as possible so I can plan the rest of the evening." He narrowed his gaze on her. "I'll even make you breakfast."

She arched a brow. "Make it coffee, hot and strong, the way I like my men, and you're on."

He smiled. "Done. Sure you don't want breakfast? I could go run by Pike Place while you're in the shower. I honestly wasn't even sure if you'd still have company when I came over this morning."

She shook her head, that sad loneliness seeping into her gaze he'd seen too many times before. "He didn't stay."

Grayson pursed his lips, unable to hide his irritation. The men she chose to keep company with were losers. Most were barely out of college and still sowing their wild oats, which meant when they were done with her, they went on their merry way. He couldn't remember the last time she'd told him one actually *had* stayed. "You deserve better, you know."

Cassie folded her arms and her gaze shifted to something behind him. She stood for a moment and stared with sightless eyes, looking suddenly lost and exposed. The same expression rose every time he brought up the subject. Cassie put on a strong show for the world, but beneath her bravado lay a soft heart, one she didn't show to many people. And this was a sore subject for them. Cassie had a reason she kept her heart under lock and key. Before he'd deployed, her boyfriend Tyler had asked her to marry him. She'd turned him down, because his job scared the hell out of her.

Grayson recalled the exact conversation, when she'd shown up at his place at eight o'clock at night, beside herself. She'd paced his living room. *I can't be that soldier's wife, Gray, who waits and worries, her insides tied in knots, wondering if her husband will come home this time.*

The announcement that Tyler had gone missing in action

hit her hard. When he was officially declared him dead a year after he went missing, Cassie drew into herself. Three years later, she still hadn't gotten over his death.

As if she'd caught herself drifting, her gaze snapped to his again, and she jabbed a pointed finger at him. "No lectures about my bad taste in men. Not all of them are like you."

He reached up and thumbed her chin. "At some point, Cass, you have to let him go and forgive yourself. You deserve to be happy, too."

She sighed, the fight draining out of her. "I'm not sure I do. He died thinking he was little more than my latest boy toy, Gray, because that was what I essentially told him. I can't forgive myself for that. Besides, this isn't about me. This is about you." She hiked her chin to a stubborn angle and flashed him a brilliant smile. "I'm not going to rain on your parade. You make me coffee, and I'll go shower."

"Deal."

She hugged him again. "I'm so damn happy for you. One of us needs to be. I'll be quick."

He knew she wouldn't be. Cassie didn't go anywhere without doing her hair and makeup. Which meant an hour passed before she emerged again. He was surfing the Web on his phone, reading the latest news, when she finally pranced back into the room, hair perfectly arranged to look like she'd merely run her fingers through it, makeup done to look "natural."

He shook his head. "You recall me telling you that the man you end up with would need deep pockets? I take that back. The man you end up with also needs patience. And lots of it. We're just going to your shop, Cass, not some elite party."

She pursed her lips, shooting him a glare. "Coffee?"

He nodded in the direction of her kitchen, around the corner. "Just finished brewing." He called out to her as she pivoted and hightailed it into the kitchen. "You're welcome."

She mumbled something he couldn't make out, though if he knew her it was likely some form of playful insult. He went back to reading his article. Ten minutes later, she emerged again, her designer stilettos arriving in his line of sight. "Okay, I'm ready."

He took a moment to close the app he'd been searching and lock his display before he looked up at her. She stood before him with a pastry in one hand and a travel mug in the other.

He furrowed his brow in disapproval at her choice of nourishment. "I could have made you a healthier breakfast than that, you know."

Her face twisted in disgust as she bit down on the icing-covered sugar bomb in her hand. "What, that vegan crap you eat? No thanks."

This made him smile. It was another long-standing argument between them. Most women he knew ate like birds. Cassie ate like she'd die tomorrow, with seemingly little care for things like cholesterol. "I'm not vegan, and they're called vegetables. You ought to try them sometime. That sugar will have you crashing in less than two hours."

She grinned and lifted her coffee mug in salute. "Which is why I have caffeine. Good coffee, by the way."

She winked and strode for the front door like a woman on a mission, heels click-clacking across her immaculately polished hardwood floors. "Come on. Before my sugar high wears off."

* * *

"Sooo...." Hannah grinned at her over the counter. "How'd last night go?"

Maddie couldn't stop the hot flush from rising into her cheeks. She waved a nonchalant hand and went back to lining the books on the window display. The latest erotic bestseller. People clamored for it, so despite the fact that their specialty was old and rare books, they opted to carry this one as well. They'd carried the first four in the series, and repeat customers had come back for the next. "It went good. We ate, we chatted, I spent the night..."

"Oh my God," Hannah squealed, coming up behind Maddie at a fast pace. "Deets, babe. Give me the deets."

"It was...hot. Grayson is Grayson, and he charmed me right of my panties."

She darted a glance at Hannah, who grinned from ear to ear. "So, *does* he look good beneath you?"

Maddie laughed. Over a year ago, they'd had a similar conversation when Hannah had been in her position. Maddie had been the one to convince her best friend to take a chance on an affair, with Cade. Hannah had asked her then: if she could do that weekend with Grayson over again, would she? Maddie had given her a flippant reply meant to disguise her true feelings. *"Maybe if I could tape his mouth shut. He could just…lie there and look pretty."*

Hannah had seen right through her, of course.

"I didn't tape his mouth shut. I rather like his mouth. But he did tie my hands, and yes, he looks very pretty beneath me." Maddie rolled her eyes. "God, Han, his body has changed. Muscles on top of muscles and washboard abs."

Hannah waved a hand. "Wait, wait, wait, back up a step. He tied you up? Seriously?"

Maddie shook her head. Her face had to be as red as a tomato by now, because she was a thousand degrees and burning up fast. "Let's just say it was his idea of a trust-building exercise. Apparently, he has a kinky side I did *not* see coming. I have to hand it to him, though. It was incredible."

"Good for you. So, you're seeing him again, I take it?"

Maddie nodded. "Tonight. He suggested dinner and a movie, but I'm not sure I care what we do. We could sit at his place and watch the news for all I care." She sighed. "I'm kind of grateful you and Christina forced me into this."

Hannah's smile came out again, this one soft and pleased and heartfelt. "It's working again. Between you two, I mean."

Maddie couldn't help the dreamy sigh that escaped her. "Yeah. It's still there. Like it never left. Like we're picking up where we left off."

Hannah nudged her shoulder. "You're in love with him."

Maddie dropped her gaze to the display. "I'm not sure I ever stopped, but yeah. I'm falling hard all over again, and it honestly scares the crap out of me. Part of me is still waiting for the other shoe to drop, but I'm not allowing myself to overthink it."

Hannah gave a decisive nod. "Good."

Maddie flashed a sheepish grin. "I'm thinking of going to Victoria's Secret and buying something sexy. Do you care if I take an hour off to run over there?"

"Nope. We're slow. Go now. I'll finish setting that up." Hannah winked at her. "Get something naughty."

"Thanks."

Maddie grabbed her purse from behind the counter and exited the shop, whistling an upbeat tune she'd heard on the radio that morning as she made the six block trek. Three blocks from her destination, a couple emerged, arm in arm, from the doorway of an expensive jewelry shop. They halted on the sidewalk in front of her and turned to each other, giving Maddie their profiles.

She came to a dead halt as recognition dawned. Grayson. With another woman. Her heart launched into her throat and blood *whoosh*ed in her ears. For several moments she could do little more than stand there and stare. Surely it wasn't what it seemed, but they related to each other with familiarity. The woman stood intimately close, her eyes illuminated as she smiled up at him. She was gorgeous, too. Small, standing a good head and shoulders below him, with a tiny, curvy figure. She had dark hair, cut in a cute, short style, with side-swept bangs that fell over her forehead. Her dress showed off her tiny waistline, and the short, flowy hem accented her shapely calves.

What got her, though, was the gleam in the woman's eyes

as she peered up at Grayson. They were too far down for Maddie to hear much more than the general hum of their voices, but his lips moved as he said something. He must have made some sort of joke, for the woman tipped her head back and laughed, then playfully swatted his chest.

They clearly knew each other well. The woman lifted onto her tiptoes to wrap her arms around his neck. Grayson bent, wrapped her in his embrace and returned the hug. He turned his head, murmuring something in her ear, then kissed her cheek before releasing her. When the woman disappeared into the store again, Grayson pivoted in Maddie's direction, only to come to an abrupt halt. Panic flashed in the depths of his widened eyes as his gaze landed on her.

Tears flooded her eyes, a vise clenched at her chest. After everything she'd shared with him, all her secrets and her fears, he'd lied to her. Again. He'd told her he had something to do. She'd assumed he meant grocery shopping or something, but clearly she'd been wrong. It wasn't some*thing* but some*one*.

Her face grew hot, and a thick lump formed in her throat. Her chest clenched with the hurt reverberating through her. What a gullible fool she'd been to ever think he was different, that he really had changed. But he hadn't. It was just lies on top of lies, and she'd been naïve enough to believe him.

Dejection sank over her. Like it had with Matt. She'd let him into her life, had happily gone with him to that party. Because she'd trusted him.

And here she was, ready to give Grayson her heart again. She should have known last night was too good to be true.

Grayson shook his head and stepped in her direction, fear rising in his eyes. "Maddie, it's not what it looks like…"

Those words from his mouth hit like a slap in the face, confirming what her heart told her. She blinked back the tears threatening to spill over.

"Go to hell, Grayson." She glared at him, then pivoted, stalking back the way she'd come as fast as she could without resorting to running. Running would look desperate. Then he'd know he'd gotten to her. And she couldn't—wouldn't!—let him know he'd hurt her, that he'd broken her. No man would ever know he'd broken her, not ever again.

She'd only gone a few steps before Grayson appeared in front of her, forcing her to halt or plow right into him. His brow was furrowed, those chocolate eyes full of regret and searching her face. "Would you stop and listen?"

A single tear escaped her tight control, leaking down her cheek, but Maddie swiped it away with a dash of her hand. "To what? More lies? I trusted you. God, what a naïve fool I've been. All you've ever done is lie to me, but I had myself convinced you were different now."

She stepped around him, but Grayson grabbed her arm, stopping her retreat, and pulled her back to him.

"Goddamn it, Maddie, for once in your life will you just listen?" He glared right back at her. "You always go off half-cocked, without bothering to talk to me first. It really sucks, you know that? You keep saying you trust me, but clearly you don't."

Her lower lip wobbled, and despite her best effort, the tears slipped out, one by one leaking down her cheeks. "I not blind, Grayson. I saw you! Any fool within three blocks can see the way she adores you." She shook off his hand. "Let go of me. She can have you, because I'm done playing your fool."

He flinched as if she'd slapped him and drew up straight. Tension radiated off him and his jaw tightened.

"Well, I should hope she's fond of me." He threw a hand in the direction of the store, behind them. "That was Cassie. God, as far as we've come, clearly we still have a long way to go. The hard part is, I can't blame you. I've made mistakes I can't take back. You're right. I should've been a little more honest, clued you in on my plans, but I didn't want to ruin it. But Cassie's right. After all the lies I've told you in the past, even a small one could end us up right back here. She's been trying to warn me this whole time, and I didn't listen."

He dragged both hands through his hair, holding long bangs back off his forehead, and stood staring at her. After a long moment, he dropped his arms to his sides, dejection rising over him. His shoulders rounded as he blew out a defeated breath.

"Trust is a decision, Maddie. You have to be willing to meet me halfway, to decide once and for all whether or not you truly forgive me for the past and are willing to give me the benefit of the doubt sometimes. We can't move forward until you do. But that's a decision only you can make." He started moving again, walking backward down the sidewalk the way he'd come. "I love you, Maddie. You're it for me. So if you decide this is something you truly want, I'll be waiting. You know where to find me."

Chapter Twelve

Maddie opened her door later that evening to find the woman she'd seen with Grayson earlier waiting out in the hallway—the absolute last person she wanted to see. To find on her doorstep the woman who only hours ago had been competition, made her heart sink into her toes. She looked as perfect as the first time Maddie had seen her, too, with her cute, short hair and flawless makeup. Her floral print skirt showed off toned thighs and calves, and was topped by a baby pink tank that hugged a lot more than Maddie's sorry little handful.

She made Maddie want to hide in a closet. In a pair of faded jeans and a T-shirt, with no bra and no makeup to speak of, she felt ugly and plain in comparison. Her only saving grace at this point was that the woman was clearly nervous. Her brow puckered with anxiety and her hands were knotted together so tightly her knuckles had turned white.

Before Maddie could think of what to say, the woman extended her arm, holding out a card that trembled in the air. "I'm not who you think I am."

Maddie glanced at the card. A business card. *Creations by Cassie* adorned the top in fancy lettering, and below that there was an address Maddie realized belonged to the exact shop where she'd seen her and Grayson.

The woman pulled her hand back, took a moment to stuff the card into the oversized Gucci handbag hanging off her right shoulder, and came out with another card. This one was her driver's license. She held it out long enough for Maddie to read her name. "I thought maybe we could talk."

Maddie's heart sank into her toes. This, apparently, really was Grayson's Cassie. A sick sensation twisted in her stomach. Grayson's words earlier had left her speechless. The hurt written on his face had haunted her all day. The woman clearly was who she said she was. Had Maddie judged him unfairly? Allowed her fear to convince her—again—of something that wasn't true?

Maddie wrapped her arms across her stomach, her chest clenching with regret. She had. She'd done it again. And here was Cassie, extending an olive branch Maddie didn't think she deserved. She wasn't sure she'd have come over appearing quite so friendly if she'd been Cassie. "About?"

Cassie released a heavy breath and folded her hands again. "I told Gray he needed to introduce us earlier, that it likely wouldn't look right to you, given…everything, but Gray…" She rolled her eyes. "He's stubborn, and he has his own agenda. He's also afraid."

Yeah, she'd heard that before. She should've listened. "Of what?"

Cassie's features seemed almost somber. "Losing you. It scares the hell out of him. To the point that he does stupid stuff in a desperate attempt to hold on to you."

Maddie let the stiffness drop out of her shoulders. "You know, it bothers me more than a little that I don't even know you."

"I know and I have no idea why, but it's partly why I'm here. To be honest, I'd wring his neck if I thought it would do any good. I told him this latest charade was a bad idea. We girls don't like discovering we've been lied to. It creates an air of distrust. The first time was good intentions gone bad. Somebody sabotaged him, and he was afraid if he told you the truth you'd end your relationship. I told him lying to you after that was a bad idea but, well, Gray's stubborn. He was also desperate." Cassie shook her head. "To say he missed you these last three years would be an understatement."

"Oh, sure, butter me up." Maddie rolled her eyes but Cassie's words got to her. Grayson had told her something similar, and the knowledge did what it always did: seeped inside and wormed its way into all those places desperately in love with him. Her heart ached with the knowledge that she'd hurt him again.

Cassie stepped forward and laid a hand on her arm.

"No, I'm serious. He's in love with you." She hesitated, looked down and shook her head before looking up again. "God, he'll kill me for telling you this, but he was shopping for jewelry this morning. For you. It's what I do. I design jewelry. He's a good guy, Maddie. A little misguided, maybe, but deep down where it counts? He's gold."

Maddie didn't know what to say that. There was so much she didn't know about him, things he hadn't shared, and standing in front of her was a woman who probably knew everything. The knowledge ate at her in a way that didn't make her very proud; there was a hard knot of ugliness caught in her chest. She wasn't a jealous person. She just wanted to stop being lied to.

Maddie furrowed her brow and shook her head, helpless. "Why did you come? I wouldn't have if I were you."

Cassie tugged on one of Maddie's hands and squeezed her fingers. "Because he's miserable, and I can't stand him when he's miserable. He's an ornery buzzard. I don't know whether to hug him or strangle him." She let out a quiet laugh then sobered. "I also came because I've been you."

Her eyes filled with an aching sadness that hit Maddie where it hurt. She stepped back, moving out of the doorway. "Come in."

Fifteen minutes later they sat at the kitchen table, two cups of hot coffee in hand. Across from her, Cassie took a sip, peering over her cup.

"I won't tell you I don't love him, because I do, but not like that. Never like that. I think he had a crush on me in high school when we first met. He even kissed me once, in college. He came to see me for spring break, and we were both bombed at the time. We laughed afterwards, in hysterics, actually, because there was no spark. It was like kissing my brother. I've never looked at him that way." Cassie sipped her coffee again before setting her cup on the table. "But I do love him, and I want him to be happy, and you make him happy."

Maddie rose from her seat, using the excuse of topping off her half-full cup in order to avoid Cassie's direct stare. "So, what you're essentially telling me is I screwed up. Again. I've done it to him again, and this time I made him leave me."

The thought went round and round in her head, taunting her, and tears flooded her eyes. Their entire relationship was in shambles, and the fault lay solely on her shoulders. The thought alone made her want to sit down and weep.

Cassie's chair scraped the floor behind her. A second later Cassie's subtle, floral scent floated around her, and a gentle hand touched her shoulder. "I won't give him this one. He made sure nothing he told you was a lie, so he's right on that front, but I can't blame you for not trusting him. I'm just saying that sometimes, when you love someone enough, you do things you regret out of fear."

Cassie's touch left her shoulder, and Maddie turned, watching as the other woman moved around the island and into the living room. Cassie stared out the window, sadness hanging on her.

"I had a Gray once. Tyler was everything to me, and I lost him." She sniffled and ducked her head, swiping her fingers beneath her eyes. "Trust me. You'll regret not having Gray more than you'll ever regret loving him."

Maddie sighed, the heavy decision pressing her down, and wrapped her arms around herself as if, somehow, she could hold all the pieces together that wanted to come apart. "This whole conversation has me sick to my stomach."

Cassie looked back over her shoulder, giving Maddie a soft smile. "I understand that, believe it or not. What it's like to have trouble trusting people. Which is why I'm here. Not to stick up for him. Grayson can hold his own. He's pissed right now, but I think it's mostly at himself. No, I'm here because I thought it might be better if we met without Gray in the picture. The look on your face when you opened the door also confirmed something for me. You love him, too."

"Yes." She couldn't deny it at this point. She had to hand it to Cassie. She was handling this way better than Maddie had.

Cassie patted her arm and strode for the front door. "I'll leave you alone now. Just think about it."

"You said he was with you today because he was purchasing something. For what?"

Cassie stopped in the foyer and turned. She frowned, her bow-shaped mouth turning down at the corners. "I've said too much as it is. I'll just tell you this. I told you Tyler was my everything? I'm fairly certain you're Gray's."

She left the apartment, closing the door softly behind her.

* * *

Grayson froze in the doorway, one hand still holding the doorknob. His heart hammered. When the doorbell had rung a minute ago he'd expected to find Cassie, come to insert her wisdom into his business again.

Instead, Maddie stood before him. She looked like hell, too. No makeup and red-rimmed eyes. The sight of her hit him like a meaty fist slammed into his gut. Leaving her had been the hardest thing he'd ever done, but standing on that sidewalk, seeing the hurt rise over her—it hit him hard where they'd ended up.

He'd spent the first two hours after leaving Maddie on the street hashing out the whole thing with Cassie, talking out everything that happened between him and Maddie over the course of their entire relationship. He'd made mistakes. Big ones. Cassie was right. This latest charade, pretending to be someone else, had done nothing but cause more problems. Except he couldn't get past one thing: It hurt, more than a little, to think she thought him capable of cheating.

He folded his arms. "Hey."

She wiped her palms several times on her jeans and looked down at the deck. At a little after three, the afternoon was surprisingly quiet. The lake's gentle waves rocked the dock beneath them; the soft sounds filling the neighborhood with a quiet serenity. The stillness contrasting with the tension all but crackled in the air between them. "I won't stay long. I didn't come to bother you. I just came to apologize."

"For?"

She let out a bitter laugh and shook her head. "Geez, where do I start? For thinking the worst of you. For not trusting you. For not listening. But mostly, for hurting you."

"I appreciate the sentiment, thank you." It was all he could say. He *did* appreciate the sentiment. He appreciated, too, that she'd come all the way out here to say it to his face, but it didn't change things. She didn't trust him, deep down, and until she did, there wasn't a thing he could do about it.

When he didn't say anything, tears filled her eyes, and her lower lip wobbled. Her throat bobbed, and her fingers trembled as she clasped her hands together.

"Cassie came to see me. I like her. She's down to earth. I don't know what I expected from her, but…talking with her made me realize something." She stopped to swallow again, and when she spoke, her voice cracked. "I'm the reason this doesn't work."

Damn it all to hell. Did she know she had him eating out of the palm of her hand? That he was two desperate little seconds from dragging her into his arms for the need to make her stop crying?

"It hurts that you even think I'm capable of cheating on you, that you think I would *ever* do that to you." It was the only card he had to play at this point, but it was the truth, and he needed her to know.

She sighed and looked up. "This isn't an excuse, more of an explanation, but…you can't tell me that if I suddenly started hanging with Cade or Sebastian you'd be okay with that. If some other guy put his hands on me, hugged me, kissed my cheek."

Okay, she had him there. Every time she'd called him Dave during their chats it had turned his insides to knots. It hadn't mattered that he knew *he* was Dave. The thought of her in another man's arms made him want to put his fist through something.

"No. You're right. I probably wouldn't be comfortable with that, but I'd trust *you*." He touched the tip of his index finger to her chest.

Maddie froze, staring at him, so still even her breathing seemed to halt. As if she were working it all out in her head. Slowly her eyes filled with more tears. How many had she shed in the last few hours? Maddie was a strong woman. To see her so open and exposed and clearly hurting cut him deep.

She blinked a few times and diverted her gaze to the deck. Defeat and dejection rounded her shoulders.

She sniffled, nodded, and reached up to swipe the back of a shaky finger beneath her right eye. "You're right. Trust is apparently a bigger issue for me than I assumed. I think maybe you're better off without me." She looked up, her gaze pausing on his for a split second, then she hiked her chin a notch. "I didn't come here to bother you. I just wanted to apologize. I'll leave you alone now. Good-bye, Grayson."

Before he could react, she pivoted and marched down the deck like she couldn't get away fast enough. Watching her hightail it away from him, his heart caught in this throat, and the words bubbled out before he'd even thought about what he *wanted* to say to her.

"You don't want to know what *I* think?"

She halted dead in her tracks at the end of the dock but didn't turn around. "No. I can see it on your face. You can call me a coward if you want, but I have no desire to hear you tell me how much I screwed up. I'm very aware right now how much I've lost, and I have to somehow figure out how to live with that. I can't change the past or alter the things I've done."

"Duly noted, but I'm going to say it anyway. For the record, I don't."

She looked back over her shoulder, brow puckered in helpless confusion. "You don't what?"

"Think I'm better off without you."

She dropped her face into her hands, her shoulders shaking as she sobbed, and some part of his brain told him to stop talking. He was airing his relationship problems to his damn neighbors, for crying out loud, but his mouth kept opening and words kept leaving.

"I'm also angry at myself. Cassie's right. This last charade was a bad fucking idea all around. Our relationship started on a lie and all I did was compound it and prove that you can't trust me." He paused to take a breath, to judge her reaction, but she didn't move. She was sobbing into her hands, and watching her was a knife to his heart. So, he kept talking, scrambling to get the words out before she walked away again. "I don't think I'm better off without you, because I've tried that, and you know what? It flat out sucks."

This time she turned to face him and all the air left his lungs. She looked like hell standing there. So goddamn defeated. She didn't move to wipe away the tears streaming down her face, but stood staring at him like she couldn't believe he'd said what he had. Her heart was in those pale blue eyes. For a moment, he couldn't breathe, couldn't seem to make his brain function long enough to drag in oxygen. His chest tightened and all he could focus on were those damn tears.

Her lower lip wobbled, another tear streaking down her cheek. "I never meant to hurt you."

"Me either." He was trying to focus on drawing a breath. If he so much as moved, if he did more than stand there and drag in oxygen, he'd be down the dock wrapping himself around her. "But we still ended up here."

She drew a shuddering breath. "I didn't come here to play the blame game, Gray. That wasn't my intention. You have every right to be angry with me. I don't expect you to forgive me, either. I just needed to say the words, because I needed you to know. I was wrong. I'm the reason this"—she lifted a hand, gesturing between them—"doesn't work."

He sighed. He'd sworn to himself he'd wait for her to come to him, when she was ready, but how the hell could he not touch her when she stood in front of him, in tears no less, taking the blame for their entire relationship's failure?

He couldn't. Damned if he could leave her standing out there all by herself.

He dropped his arms to his sides, gave in to the pull of her, and nodded in the direction of the interior of the house behind him. "Would you like to come in?"

She wrapped her arms around herself and shook her head. "I don't want to intrude."

He held out a hand. He'd meant the gesture as a halfway point, an olive branch. At the very least, he wanted to clear the air between them. Wherever their relationship went from here, he didn't want there to be hurt and anger left between them.

Except she crossed the space between them, set her hand hesitantly in his and her body hit his before he even realized he'd pulled her in. He wrapped an arm around her and her hand settled on his chest, warming his skin through his T-shirt. Relief shuddered through him.

More of those damn tears filled her eyes, and her lower lip trembled. "I swear I never meant to hurt you."

He stroked his hand over her back, glorifying in the simple fact that he could touch her at all, in the feel of her body beneath his fingers. "Me, either."

"What happens now?"

He nodded again toward the interior of the house. "You could come in."

She dropped her gaze to his chest. "Do you want me to?"

More than he could possibly tell her. Instead of answering, though, he slipped his hand into hers and tugged her past the threshold, closing the door behind her. Then he moved to the couch, took a seat and pulled her onto his lap. She sat stiffly before snuggling into him and laying her head on his shoulder. She wrapped her arms around his waist and pressed her face into his neck. Warm wetness trailed over his skin, disappearing beneath the neck of his shirt.

So he wrapped his arms around her in turn, hugging her tightly to him, and stroked her back. "Please don't cry, baby. God, I hate seeing you cry."

She sniffled and drew a shaky breath, lifting one hand to

wipe her face. "I'm sorry. It's all I've done for three hours now."

He hadn't a clue what happened now, but he had to be honest with her. "I meant it when I said I loved you, you know. I was very angry with you earlier, but I am madly in love with you."

"Was?"

He let out a heavy breath, releasing the last of his frustration with it. Okay, so he was a sap and a sucker for tears. "Yeah. I'll admit I'm starting to cool off. That you came over here means a lot. It tells me that despite your nuttiness…"

She clearly caught the tease in his tone, because she poked him in the ribs. "Hey…"

He flinched away from her touch and let out a soft laugh. "*It tells me* that you care, too. And let's face it. You in tears isn't something I can handle. The fact remains, though, baby, you don't trust me."

Her head rocked against his shoulder.

"It isn't you I don't trust. I've never had anything like this. After my rape in college, I went in the exact opposite direction. I closed myself off. I meant it when I told Dave he was a first for me in a long time. You were my first and my last, Gray. Since college, I haven't really dated." Several seconds of silence passed. When she spoke again, her voice was small and meek, and she went still against him. "I was afraid to trust, afraid of getting hurt again. I kept waiting for the other shoe to drop, so when I saw you with her, I just assumed…"

He kissed the top of her head. "I would never do that to

you. I'm not perfect, and God knows I've made my share of mistakes, but that's not me."

She sniffled again. "I'm sorry."

He tightened his hold on her, leaning his head against hers. "Me too, baby."

She snuggled deeper into him, and he reveled in the simplicity of holding her.

"I love you too, you know," she whispered from his throat. "Loving you makes me nuts. I'm pretty sure I'm the girlfriend from hell, but I do love you. I'm not sure I know how to live without you. These last three years, I've really missed you. I tried to convince myself I didn't feel it, but I've been miserable. I came over because the thought of losing you again the same way made my chest hurt."

He lifted his head and peered at her. "Look at me." He waited until her gaze met his, then pressed his nose to hers. "I'm not going anywhere. Got that?"

She smiled, tears flooding her eyes again, and touched his cheek, caressing him with her fingertips. "I have no idea why, but I'm damn grateful."

He playfully rolled his eyes. "Because I'm addicted to you. Because I don't know how to live without you, either."

His thoughts went to the little surprise he'd planned, the entire reason he'd gone shopping that morning. If he knew Cassie, she'd no doubt spilled the beans.

He sighed. "I suppose Cassie told you what we were doing this morning?"

Maddie hitched a shoulder, her gaze dropping to his chest. Her fingers stroked along the collar of his shirt, grazing his skin. "She mentioned you were shopping for jewelry."

He furrowed his brow, glaring at the picture of Cassie that popped into his thoughts. "I'm going to have to remember to kill her. Would you like to see what I bought?"

"Don't kill her. She meant well. And I only want to see if you want to share."

"I want to share, but I'll need to get up. It's upstairs in my dresser." He tucked two fingers beneath her chin, lifting her mouth for a kiss, then picked her up and deposited her onto the couch beside him. After pushing to his feet, he pointed a finger at her. He aimed for stern, but his heart was too light and his nerves too scattered. His lips curled, betraying him. "Don't. Move."

Maddie didn't smile. Rather, she stared at him with somber eyes. "I'm not going anywhere. I promise. I'm done running, Gray. I need you too much."

He bent over, whispering as he brushed another kiss across her mouth. "God, I can't resist you. Ditto, baby."

"Does this mean you forgive me?" Her heart was in her widened eyes, as if somehow she still feared he'd say no.

He stroked her cheek with the backs of his fingers. "Can you forgive *me*?"

Relief moved over her features, softening the stiff set of her shoulders. She smiled, the awful anxiety leaving her eyes. "Already have."

"Good. Wait here." He pecked her lips then jogged through the living room and bounded up the stairs two at a time. As he moved down the hallway into his bedroom, his nerves settled in his stomach. He pulled the black ring box out of the top drawer of his dresser and held it in his shaking palm. She was a first in so many ways. He'd never proposed to someone before. God, if she said no…

Disregarding the thought as quickly as it formed, he closed the drawer and jogged back downstairs. Standing in front of her again, his heart launched into his throat. She smiled and blinked, her expression tender but clueless.

He tightened his fingers around the box, using its solidity to get him past the nerves. He'd bought this ring with her mind. It wasn't a traditional solitaire, because Maddie wasn't a traditional girl. Cassie had chosen it, and he agreed. The emeralds on either side of the diamond would set off Maddie's fiery hair. The twisted band was intricately carved. The ring would look beautiful on her finger.

He took a deep breath. Here went nothing.

He arched a brow, aiming for teasing, although his stomach was doing somersaults.

"I had plans, you know. I wanted to make a grand gesture you'd never forget, but since you waylaid that…" He playfully narrowed his eyes. Maddie's cheeks flushed a deep crimson, but one corner of her mouth hitched. "But if I'm going to do this, I'm doing it right."

"Okay…" She nodded but once again blinked up at him like she hadn't a clue what he meant. Was it possible she didn't? How could she not? Maybe Cassie hadn't spilled the beans entirely.

He sucked in another deep breath for courage, sent up a silent prayer that the words he'd practiced would magically form on his tongue, then dropped to one knee in front of her. He held out his hand, opening his fist, and opened of the lid of the box.

Maddie gasped, her shaking hands flying to cover her mouth. "Oh God. Cassie only said you were shopping for jewelry. Oh God…"

Grayson let out a nervous laugh. Here he was, his heart hammering so hard he feared the damn thing would burst from his chest, and she stared at the box in his hands like she truly hadn't a clue. "What did you expect?"

She giggled behind her hand, eyes already tearing up, and shook her head. Her voice came out muffled behind her trembling fingers.

"I don't know. Cassie didn't say what kind of jewelry, and I thought about that bracelet you gave me three years ago…" She let out a nervous laugh, then dropped her hands from her mouth and narrowed her eyes. "I was too focused on the fact that your other woman had shown up on my doorstep."

Grayson swallowed a groan. She'd never let him live that down. "Cassie is not my other woman. I kissed her once. In college. I'll give you that. But it was like kissing my sister."

Maddie's eyes gleamed, sparking with amusement. "She mentioned that."

He groaned. "Baby, you're killing me here. I had this whole speech I memorized…"

She dropped her hands to her lap and sat up straight. "I'm sorry. Continue."

"Thank you." One corner of his mouth quirked upward with nervous relief, but one look at her face and he was lost in her eyes and the words left his mouth of their own accord. "I love you, Maddie. I knew I loved you long before we broke up. That was part of what I wanted to tell you that weekend, and I've spent the last three years trying to figure out how on earth I was going to live without you. So, I fully admit pretending to be someone else for that auction wasn't the brightest idea I've ever had, but it brought you back to me, and I can't be sorry for that."

Tears welled in her eyes. "Me, either."

He shifted onto both knees and shuffled toward her, edging between her thighs until they were nose to nose, and he took every breath with her. His proposal had to be a damn cliché, but he was lost in her incredible eyes. God, she really was his. "You're it for me, Maddie. I told you. I'm not letting you go again. Ever. Marry me?"

His breath halted as he waited for her reply. Apparently, she decided to torture him, because the long moment passed in unbearable silence. Tears leaked down her cheeks one by one, and her throat bobbed, but Maddie just sat blinking. He waited her out.

Finally, she reached out, caressing his cheek with her warm palm. "That's the sweetest thing any man has ever said to me."

He pulled the ring from the box, and when she held out her trembling hand, he slid it onto her finger. It looked perfect on her.

"It's really beautiful, Gray." She stared down at her hand. Seconds later, she looked up and launched out of her seat, hurling herself against him with a force that sent them sprawling to the floor. He let out an *ooof* as she landed on top of him, but his temporary surprise became lost as she rained kisses over his face. She pecked his cheeks, his forehead, his nose. Several landed on his mouth.

He wrapped his arms around her and chuckled. "Is that your way of saying yes?"

She let out a watery laugh and lifted her head enough to meet his gaze. "That's an ecstatic yes."

More grateful than he had words for, he crushed her to him and captured her mouth. For a moment, he allowed himself to luxuriate in the way her lips melted over his. Her tongue slid against his, her fingers dove into his hair, and he curved his hands around her bottom, drawing her tighter against him. Thoughts of stripping her bare and making love to her right there on the floor began to take root when she pulled her mouth from his as if something had suddenly occurred to her.

Her brow furrowed, her breathing as ragged as his. "You said you had plans. What were you going to do?"

He blew out a disappointed breath and dropped his head to the floor, forcing his mind to focus. Damned if his hands would stop wandering, though. He couldn't resist squeezing her ass, running his hands up her sides and grazing her breasts. Any part of her he could reach, he ached to touch. Simply because he could.

"I was going to put an ad in the paper. Front page. Since that damn paper is the reason we broke up, I thought it suited. Something positive to counteract the negative. Plus, it's something we'd be able to keep."

She smiled, eyes twinkling in amusement. "You're just a big softie, aren't you?"

"Guilty as charged." He grinned and sat up, rolled her over and settled onto his elbows. He stroked his fingers through the strands of hair falling around her shoulders. "Will you stay tonight?"

She nodded and slid her hands up his back, burrowing beneath his T-shirt. Her fingers were warm and supple against his skin. "I'll stay."

"Good. I want to spend the night making love to every inch of you. I want to see how many times I can make you scream my name before you wave the white flag. I'm going to start with my mouth." He dipped his head, demonstrating what he had in mind by following the line of her jaw with his tongue.

She shuddered, exhaling a shaky breath.

"Then maybe I'll use my fingers." This time, he slid a hand over her right breast, thumbing her distended nipple.

She rewarded him with a gasp.

"And my cock." He arched his hips against her, thrusting into the softness of her belly.

This time, they both groaned. Christ, she felt good. It had only been four hours, but it felt like forever, and he was too aware of how close he'd come to losing her for good. His chest filled with a desperate need to fuse with her, to get as close to her as he could for as long as he could.

"Uh-uh." Despite her denial, her voice was a breathy whisper, her body already trembling beneath him. "It's my turn."

That caught him. He paused at the edge of her earlobe. It took a moment for the fog to recede enough for him to recall what she meant. He'd promised her she could tie him up and have her way with him. The thought alone had his cock hardening to the point of pain.

"Not tonight." He shook his head and closed his mouth over her earlobe, sucking on it gently. "I want to take my time with you tonight. You can tie me up another time. After I've had my fill of you. Next week sometime."

Maddie went still and silent beneath him. Concentrating now on the curve of her jaw, he waited her out, contenting himself with seeking out every place she'd dotted her perfume. Or maybe it was body wash, because the coconut scent seemed to emanate from everywhere, as if it was embedded in her skin. All that scent did was make him hungry, he yearned to discover the intimate scent of her, to burrow his mouth between her thighs. He had yet to taste her, and God how he ached to.

When she didn't say anything, he lifted his head. Her wide-eyed expression had his breath halting in his lungs. Her gaze roved his face, searching and anxious. It didn't escape his notice that her chest rose and fell at a more rapid pace.

He stroked his fingers over her cheek. "Okay, that look on your face scares me. Tell me."

"Would you think I was crazy if I said I didn't want to wait?"

He allowed himself to breathe again and stroked her hair back off her forehead. "To get married?"

"Yes."

"No. The sooner we get married, the sooner you're mine." He nipped at her bottom lip, but she didn't respond the way he expected. Rather than kissing him back, her gaze remained somber.

One hand slid between them, and her palm settled over his left shoulder. "I've always been yours, Gray. Just took me a while to be able to admit it."

He brushed a soft kiss across her mouth. "Ditto, baby. Took me three damn years to realize I couldn't live without you. Next weekend?"

She nodded. "Next weekend. We could do Vegas."

He frowned and shook his head, disgusted by the thought. "No. I'm not marrying you in one of those cheesy little chapels. We'll make something happen, okay?"

She smiled, relief flooding her features, and the tension drained from her body. "I was afraid you'd think we'd jumped too far in the opposite direction."

"Well, we kind of did, but I'll admit I had the same thought. I've waited three years for you to come back to me. I don't want to wait anymore to make you mine."

Her hands slid to his waist, caught the hem of his T-shirt, and pushed it up his body. "I'm glad we agree. I was thinking the same thing."

He reached back and caught his shirt in his fist, pulling it over his head. After worming his way out of it with her help, he tossed it to the floor and bent his head to her neck again, following the trail of her perfume. "Now that that's settled, where we were?"

With a wicked gleam in her eyes, she sat up then rolled

him onto his back and straddled his hips. As she settled her heat over the bulge ready to bust the seam on his jeans, she grinned. She picked up each of his hands, threading their fingers together, then pinned his arms over his head. "I believe you were just submitting to me."

Her breasts were in his face, and the hunger and predatory look in her eyes made his balls ache, but he couldn't contain the laughter that bubbled out of him. Damn, but she was feisty.

He shook his head. "God, I love you. Okay, you win. I give. I'm yours. Have your way with me, baby."

Please see the next page for a preview of the final book in JM Stewart's Seattle Bachelors series, *Claiming the Billionaire*.

Available January 2017!

Chapter One

"Cassie, honey, are you sitting down?"

Phone in one hand, pitcher of water in the other, Cassandra Stephanopoulos halted dead center of her kitchen. The coffee she'd been in the process of making went forgotten as ice skittered down her spine, plunking hard and cold in her belly and awakening her sleepy senses. Every bit of bad news she'd ever received seemed to come off the heels of a line like that.

Any other day, she didn't pick up her phone before she'd had a much needed morning dose of caffeine. Things like talking coherently simply didn't happen before coffee. She'd glanced at the screen, though. Who the hell would call her so early? Grayson and the girls all knew she wasn't a morning person.

At seeing Marilyn Benson's number, though, she'd snatched her phone off the counter. Marilyn was Tyler's mother. Cassie had dated him three years ago. She'd done what she swore to herself she wouldn't…she'd fallen for a soldier. And her worst fear had happened—Tyler never came home. Marilyn was her only connection to him now. It was a tiny, stupid little scrap to hold on to. It wouldn't bring him back, but she needed the connection like she needed oxygen.

More to the point, Marilyn had only called her this early twice: the first time to tell her Tyler had gone missing. The second…to tell her they'd called off the search for him. All of which now had Cassie's mind racing with horrible possibilities. Her hands began to shake, sending the cold water sloshing over the rim of the full pitcher and onto her bare toes.

She deposited the pitcher on the nearest counter, pinched the bridge of her nose and forced herself to count to three before answering. She would *not* allow the panic slithering up her spine to take root. "Is everything okay? Are Dean and the girls all right?"

Tyler's older brother Dean and his wife Kathy had two gorgeous little girls with the biggest blue eyes Cassie had ever seen. Every time she saw them they made her chest ache, because she always wondered. If Tyler had lived and she hadn't taken the coward's way out, would their kids have inherited those eyes as well?

"Sweetie, I have news."

The odd tone in Marilyn's voice had Cassie's stomach sinking into her toes. Now she knew the news was bad. She reached out to grip the edge of a nearby counter, and swallowed past the lump in her throat. "My stomach's in knots. Whatever it is, just tell me. Please."

On the other end of the line, Marilyn drew a shaky breath. "Sweetie, Tyler's alive."

Marilyn's voice came out barely above a whisper, but she might as well have shouted the words. Everything inside Cassie skidded to a halt. She stared out the long row of windows on the other side of her penthouse apartment. Despite it being January in Seattle, the skies were clear blue. The beauty somehow added a surreal quality to the moment. How many times had she longed for this exact phone call? Surely she was only dreaming…

"Come again?"

Marilyn laughed, the sound of someone so relieved they were beside themselves. "He's alive. I just spoke with him. He sounds a little shaky, to be honest, but he's alive. Apparently, he was held captive. I'm afraid I don't know the whole story yet, but oh, sweetie, he's coming home."

Marilyn continued to ramble, her voice a giddy, half delirious murmur on the other end of the line, but the actual words didn't register. The impact of the news struck Cassie like a wayward arrow, piercing her heart. She sagged back against the kitchen counter, staring at everything and nothing, as tears rushed over her, bringing with them a profound sense of relief.

Tyler was alive.

* * *

Cassie bee-bopped to the tune playing in her right ear as she made her way down the hotel corridor. The long hallway stood empty, save a few other last minute arrivals. Grayson, her long time best friend, and his new wife, Maddie, walked a couple steps behind, their gates more casual than Cassie's buoyant stride. It was rude to listen to music in the presence of friends, but as newlyweds, Maddie and Gray had gone off in a world of their own, and Cassie needed the upbeat tune to bolster her mood. Maybe if she forced herself to be cheerful, she'd eventually feel it.

She couldn't believe she'd let Gray talk her into this. She didn't want to be here. No, she'd rather be alone in her penthouse with a fifth of scotch, getting so drunk she couldn't remember her name. A week had passed since Marilyn had called to tell her Tyler was alive. Somehow, he'd not only managed to survive being captured in Afghanistan by the Taliban, but had gotten himself home. To say she was relieved would be the understatement of the century.

Except he hadn't come to see her. He'd been home for seven days now and he hadn't so much as called her. But why would he? After the way they'd left things, the things they'd said to each other, she certainly wouldn't come to see her either.

Exactly why she'd allowed Gray to drag her to this auction.

When the too-familiar pain began to wrap itself around her chest again, Cassie refocused on the upbeat music and paused to shimmy out the last strains of the song. She'd have fun tonight if it killed her.

Behind her, Gray chuckled. "I'm glad to see you're in a good mood tonight, Cassie. I thought you'd be pissed when I showed up earlier."

She pulled out the ear-bud and looked down at her phone, closing the music app.

"You're lucky. I've heard about these shindigs from a few friends. If I'm lucky, I'll end up with two of Christina's hotties." She shot a wink over her shoulder. "They can make me a Cassie sandwich."

Okay, so she wasn't really in the mood for company. She'd intended to spend tonight alone, wallowing in her self-pity, but Gray had waylaid those plans. He'd shown up at her place two hours ago, demanded she get dressed, and dragged her out of her apartment. He hadn't told her where they were headed until they were halfway here.

Cassie had known Christina McKenzie, now apparently Christina Blake, in high school. Christina ran a charity auction that had become famous over the last few years. This year, she'd turned the tables a bit. Instead of bachelors, they were auctioning the ladies. Three months ago, Gray had talked her into signing up as one of the bachelorettes. Up until six months ago, this would have been her style. An evening with a potentially hot guy? Yeah, she'd have been all over that. The last three years had been a series of one man after another, because she'd been determined to never again fall the way she had for Tyler. Love only led to heartbreak, and hers had only begun to heal.

She'd changed her entire outlook six months ago, though, determined to release that side of herself. Marilyn's recent phone call left her with a desperate need to fill the void opening inside of her.

Gray rolled his eyes as he came to a stop beside her. "Some things haven't changed, I see."

"Actually, I've decided you're right, Gray. This is exactly the distraction I need tonight. Besides, you only live once." She playfully nudged him with an elbow. "You should have volunteered Maddie. You can make a Maddie sandwich."

"I don't share." Gray glared at her, but the corners of his mouth twitched with his effort to hold back a grin.

Okay, so it wasn't nice to tease him, but Grayson Lockwood had been her best friend since high school—since that tenth grade English class she'd only passed because he'd taken pity on her. They teased each other as easily as they confided in each other. Besides, that's what he got for storming her apartment.

Luckily for her, the gleam in Maddie's eyes told her she'd gotten the joke. Maddie winked, covered her mouth and let out a girlish giggle. Cassie bit the inside of her cheek to keep from laughing. She and Maddie might have had a rocky start, but they were fast becoming friends. Maddie had a wicked sense of humor but a heart of gold. She also made Gray happy.

Gray jerked his gaze to his wife. "And what are *you* laughing at?"

Maddie blinked up at him, innocence personified. "What? I kind of like the idea. Didn't you say you wanted to try something different?"

Gray turned his head, shooting Cassie a glare. "Touché,

Cassandra. Touché. Consider us even now." He jerked his gaze back to Maddie. "You, however, I can spank."

When he backed Maddie against the nearest wall and set his hands on either side of her head, Cassie pivoted away from the newlyweds. She was damn happy for them. She really was. After a long, painful road that had nearly taken them away from each other and the dangerous childhood he'd endured, Gray deserved to be happy. She needed him to be.

Seeing them together, though, made her chest ache. She'd had that once, and every time they nuzzled each other only reminded her how much she missed it. She'd screwed up, plain and simple. She'd held the world in the palm of her hand and gave it up, and for what? So she could prove she didn't need anybody?

"Don't take too long. You guys only have five minutes." Cassie shot a sassy wink over her shoulder and turned, striding for the ballroom entrance at the end of the hall.

She came to a stop inside and took a moment to gather herself. She'd only get through tonight by smiling and pretending life was a party. If luck found her, maybe she'd fake herself into believing her chest wasn't caving in.

Inside, the place was more men than women, every one of them dressed to the nines. The men gorgeous and debonair in their black tuxes, the women regal and glowing in their finest gowns and jewels. Each face lit up with the promise of the evening. A feeling she wished she shared. The whole evening exhausted her. She wasn't in the mood to put on the act tonight. Her mind had gotten stuck on the fact that

Tyler was alive. She wouldn't be able to believe it until she saw him for herself, but that likely wouldn't happen.

"Don't think I didn't see what you did back there."

Gray's deep voice sounded behind her seconds before his hand settled on her shoulder, warm and heavy and supportive.

Cassie darted a glance at him. "Shouldn't you be whisking Maddie off to a dark corner somewhere?"

As if on cue, Maddie stepped up beside Gray.

"I'm going to go find Christina and say hello." Maddie lifted onto her toes, kissed him softly, and turned to Cassie. She took one of Cassie's hands, offering a sympathetic smile. "All kidding aside, I'm glad you're here. Don't be too mad at him. This part was my idea. I hated the thought of you sitting home alone, feeling miserable, so I told Gray to go over and get you. Hannah always did that for me, those three years Gray and I were apart. Forced me to get up, to live. It was hard, but she was right."

She'd come to adore Maddie. Turned out, they had a lot in common. They both had pasts they wished they could change, and like Cassie, Maddie tended to put on a front, to avoid feeling things. More to the point, what Maddie had gone through with Gray meant she understood the moment Cassie had arrived at—knowing she needed to move on, but not knowing how.

Cassie plastered on the best smile she could muster. "Thank you. I'm not mad. I'm just not sure I'm up for this."

Maddie squeezed her fingers. "Smile like it's the best night of your life. Besides, whoever it is you end up with, you're only required a single date. At the very least, he'll keep your mind off your heart."

Cassie squeezed Maddie's fingers in turn, watching her fiery hair disappear into the crowd before glancing at Gray. "I really like her. She's good for you."

She had to admit, she was grateful for a moment alone with him. Only with Gray did she feel comfortable letting down her walls. Even her father put pressure on her to be someone else. Someone more perfect. With her *baba*, nothing she did was ever enough. *"When are you going to get serious, Cassandra? You can't play like a child all your life. I'm not going to be around forever. Who will take over the restaurants when I die?"* Her father had said the words so many times she could hear his Greek accent echo in her head even now.

She was her father's biggest disappointment. He and her mother had opened Ariana's Greek Café before she and her brother Nick were born. Authentic Greek cuisine, with recipes that had been passed down for generations. She and Nick had been raised on those restaurants and Daddy insisted they learn the business, to take over when he and Mom could no longer run them. Now that they'd lost her mother and Nick, the heavy burden had fallen to her. Cassie wasn't a restaurateur. She had the soul of an artist, which displeased him no end.

Gray, though, always accepted her as she was—broken, crabby bits and all.

Gray pulled her against his side. "Maddie likes you, too. I warned her you probably wouldn't be yourself tonight."

"I appreciate it. Tell her I said thanks. I hope she knows it isn't personal." Cassie scanned the crowd again and sighed. "Remind me again why I'm here?"

What she needed tonight was a pint of Ben & Jerry's and a really big spoon.

"Because she's right. You sitting at home crying your eyes out doesn't do you any good." Gray gave her shoulders a gentle squeeze, amusement lighting his voice. "You being one of the bachelorettes gives you a purpose, something to do. Besides, raccoon eyes aren't a good look on you."

He winked, and she let out a watery laugh, but staring into the room, the weight of the entire evening pressed down on her. "I don't know how to let him go, Gray. I tried for three years. I want to have fun tonight, but I'm not sure I can. It's killing me that he hasn't even called me."

Nor did she think she deserved the happiness she coveted. She'd told Tyler she'd used him, that he was little more than her latest boy toy. She couldn't forgive herself for that, and clearly, he hadn't either.

"Let me talk to Christina. I'm willing to bet she'd know the perfect guy to fix you up with. If I know her, she knows everyone here personally. I bet she can fix you up with someone who won't expect anything from you."

Cassie rolled her eyes. "That's pathetic. I can get my own dates."

He looked over at her, one dark brow lifting in challenge. "Then why aren't you?"

"Point taken." Six months ago, when she'd stood as his "best woman" at his wedding, she'd come to the realization her life was a sham. Since Tyler's disappearance, she'd been diverting, burying herself in playing the carefree party girl, because she couldn't admit to herself his death had pulled the rug out from beneath her. When she wasn't at the jewelry shop, or designing a piece, she could usually be found in a club, or at a bar picking up the hottie-du-jour. All in the name of desperately trying not to think about Ty.

Watching Gray profess to love, honor, and cherish Maddie for the rest of his life had been an honest moment for her. She couldn't deny she wanted what they'd found. The happily ever after. Except the man she wanted it with was gone and no amount of wishing would bring him back.

She'd decided that day to stop living a lie. Her custom jewelry design had borne the brunt of her insomnia. Creations by Cassie was doing better than ever. A handful of large stores had even commissioned pieces. Some of her best work had taken shape at one in the morning, often fueled by heartache. Apparently, sleepless nights and lack of sex was good for the muse.

Tonight, she needed her carefree side or she wouldn't make it to morning without curling up into a sobbing mess. She was glad Tyler was alive. The knowledge eased a wound in her soul. A world without him in it didn't make sense. Except she now had to face losing him a second time.

She turned her head to search the ballroom, stopping when she'd found her target. "I see the bar. I'm going to get a drink before this starts. A strong one."

Gray gave her shoulder a gentle squeeze. "We'll be sitting toward the middle. They should be starting soon."

She reached back, settling her hand over his in return. "Thanks. I won't be long."

As she approached the bar, the hunky blond behind the counter flashed a thousand-watter and rested his hands on the surface. She didn't miss the appreciative gleam in his eyes as his gaze swept over her. "What can I get you, sweetheart?"

Momentarily distracted, she smiled in return. His grin could charm the panties off even the coldest woman, and with muscles on top of muscles, he looked like he could be one of Christina's bachelors. He'd no doubt been hired for that reason.

Deciding to grab the evening by its ears, to not let the pain suck her under, she pulled her "bad girl without a conscience" out of her closet. She leaned on the bar, giving Mr. Muscles the once over, along with a view of her cleavage. "Give me a Screaming Orgasm."

Okay, so she'd rather have two fingers of scotch, but flirting with Mr. Muscles over there was exactly what the doctor prescribed.

Luckily for her, he took her sassy order with good humor. He grinned, one corner of his mouth hitching higher than the other, and pulled out a tumbler. He filled it with ice, added equal parts vodka, Irish cream, and coffee liquor, and winked at her as he pushed the drink across the counter. "I get off at ten. For now, this'll have to do."

Cassie laughed. Yup. He'd definitely been hired for a purpose. No doubt he sold more liquor on his flirtatious smile alone. "You should be careful with lines like that. A lesser woman might take you up on it."

He leaned his elbows on the bar, his grin widening. "Who says it was a line?"

She laughed again and dug in her purse, pulled out a hundred-dollar bill, and stuffed it into the tip jar on the counter. "Honey, you just made my night."

Someone tapped the microphone. "Pardon the interruption, everyone. Can I have the ladies on stage, please? We'll begin in a few minutes."

"Oops, that's me." She picked up her drink off the counter and saluted him before tipping the contents into her mouth. It slid smooth and creamy down her throat, hitting her belly and warming her from the inside. It didn't thaw the ice around her heart, but it went a long way. She winked at Mr. Muscles. "Bachelorette number one."

Somewhat bolstered, she made her way onto the small stage, taking her place at the head of the line of women. Busy finding their seats, the crowd out beyond the stage wove their way through the rows of gray folding chairs. She had to hand it to them. The men were subtle, respectful. A group of women getting ready to outbid each other over hunky bachelors would have been a whole lot more raucous. Maddie, who'd attended the last three, had told her as much.

As it turned out, Gray and Maddie were seated at the end of a row in the center of it all. He caught her eye and gave her a thumbs-up. Cassie smiled in return. Yeah, she could do this.

Christina stepped up to the podium, back straight, hands resting on the wooden surface. "Thank you all for coming tonight. Welcome to the fifth annual auction for breast cancer research. Of course, we're all here for the same reason. To fight this disease. Breast cancer has claimed too many women in my family. I know some of you here tonight are survivors. I say we fight this disease with a little style. Now, every year since its inception, I've gathered Seattle's finest bachelors. This year, I thought the men deserved a little treat."

Applause erupted through the ballroom. Several whoops came from various points in the room. Christina laughed and waved her hands to quiet the crowd.

"All right, gentlemen. Allow me to introduce our first bachelorette, Miss Cassandra Stephanopoulos."

At hearing her name, Cassie drew a deep breath, straightened her shoulders, and moved toward the podium. Drawing her inner vixen around her, she plastered on her flirtiest smile and put a little extra swing in her hips. Applause once again erupted around the room. From somewhere in the back, a wolf whistle pierced the air, though the lights pointed at the stage made seeing where it had come from near impossible.

Christina turned to wink at her as she approached the podium. "It appears you already have fans."

Cassie laughed and took a bow. "Thank you. I'll be here all night."

"Gentlemen, a little about Cassie. Her father owns and runs the chain of Greek restaurants, Ariana's Greek Café. She paints and designs custom jewelry. Her shop, Creations by Cassie, sits a few blocks from here. In fact, for any ladies in attendance, she designed the necklace I'm wearing. When asked, she said she likens herself to a sorority girl—she's just out to have a little fun." Christina looked up from her cards, winking at the audience. "But don't get any ideas, guys. Her best friend is the big guy in the fifth row."

Gray stood, humor lacing his tone as he turned his head, addressing the crowd around him. "Consider me her personal bouncer."

When he bowed, Cassie playfully rolled her eyes. The crowd laughed.

Christina let out a soft laugh as well. "Actually, Cassie told me she thinks life is too short to be too serious. Isn't that right, Cassie?"

Cassie forced herself to smile and nod, but her heart ached. Tyler's death had taught her something. "I fully intend to enjoy the life I have. Live it to the fullest. Good food, good wine, good friends."

Christina wrapped an arm around her, giving her a gentle, reassuring squeeze, before turning back to the crowd. Clearly Gray had filled her in. "All right, shall we start the bidding?"

More applause came from the crowd as Christina stepped back and the auctioneer took her place at the podium. "All right, gentlemen, let's start the bidding at ten thousand…"

Several minutes passed as bids ping-ponged around the room, each one higher than the last.

"One hundred thousand." A man's voice called out from the back of the long room.

Cassie froze.

She knew that voice. She'd know it in the dead of night, in the darkest cave.

The familiar sound of it skittered down her spine, and her playful smile melted. Her hands shook at her sides. Heart hammering, she shielded her eyes, squinting against the bright lights aimed at the stage, and searched the crowd for the face to go with the voice. Even while she searched, rational thought warred with the pain still pounding around in her chest. It couldn't be Tyler. He wouldn't have come to see her. She'd hurt him too much, had looked him right in the eye and told him he meant nothing to her beyond sex. And then sent him off to die.

The room fell silent, tension rising over the space.

Christina's hand slid over her shoulder, her voice warm and low in Cassie's ear. "You're three shades of white, honey. Are you all right?"

Cassie's blood roared in her ears, pounding so hard the room began to spin, but she forced herself to smile and glanced at Christina. "I'm fine. The voice just spooked me. Sounded like someone I know."

It had to be a trick of the room. The high ceilings made the noise echo. Combined with her grief, her ears clearly played tricks on her. She was hearing things, that's all.

Christina didn't look convinced. "Are you sure?"

Cassie nodded. "I'm fine. Continue, please. I'm sorry for the interruption."

Christina smiled and the auctioneer started the bidding again. As the bids once again ping-ponged around the room, the man in back, whose voice had spooked her, countered every bid. He didn't say anything else, but raised his bidding number repeatedly. Several more minutes passed, as the bids rose higher, the number of men participating dwindling to two. Finally, when the number reached four hundred thousand, the second bidder bowed out.

"Sold. To the gentleman in the back."

As the auctioneer's voice rang through the room, the man in the back strode toward the stage. Cassie held her breath. The closer he got, the louder her heartbeat pounded in her ears. He looked like Tyler. He had the same tall build and broad shoulders, the same dark hair, cropped close per army regulation. She couldn't see the color of his eyes from this distance, though. Not to mention he looked thinner than Ty had been the last time she'd seen him. Ty had always been a big, burly guy, tall and thickly muscled. This guy was tall but lean, and he walked with a slight limp Tyler hadn't had.

When he came to a stop in front of the stage, head tipped back to peer up at her, her heart stopped altogether. Closer now, she could clearly see his eyes were blue.

Like Ty's.

Nausea swirled in her stomach, at war with the guilt, the part of her that wanted, needed, this man to be Tyler. She knew better, though…didn't she?

The room swayed as dizziness swept over her. This was wrong. This was all wrong.

She jerked her gaze to Christina. "Is this some sort of a joke?"

Christina shook her head, looking between Cassie to the audience in helpless confusion. "I have no idea what's going on, sweetie, but I assure you I had nothing to do with whatever this is."

Cassie turned to look out over the audience, her heart hammering in her ears. Marilyn's phone call came rushing back to her. *"Tyler's alive."*

She'd been waiting for this moment right here. She'd heard Marilyn's words that day, a week ago now, but hadn't truly believed them. She needed to see him.

Out in the audience, Gray pushed to his feet and strode toward the stage, his long strides closing the distance in record time. Concern etched his face.

"This isn't real. It can't be." Cassie shook her head, watching Tyler's eyes, waiting for him to explain, to say...something.

Tyler opened and closed his mouth a few times, but long moments passed in aching silence as he stared up at her with tired eyes rimmed in shadows. Finally, his throat bobbed as he swallowed. "I had to see you."

Before she could think or remember to breathe, Gray came to a stop in front of the stage. He furrowed his brow, turning to glare at Tyler. "It's fucking cruel to show up this way, man."

Tyler turned his head, glaring back. "Three years. Three fucking years sitting..." He shook his head, his face blanching, and straightened his shoulders. "I saw the commercial on TV an hour ago. So fucking sue me for needing to see her."

The sound of his voice finally rooted her in reality. The last lingering threads of denial unraveled. Tyler really was alive. As shock receded, the wall she'd put her pain behind three years ago cracked. Three years of grief flooded over her like a tidal wave, and a vise closed around her chest, threatening to pull her knees out from beneath her.

"I can't deal with this." Cassie stalked from the stage, moving as fast as she dared without resorting to running as she headed out of the ballroom. Head spinning, her stomach churning, she stalked the long hallway and jabbed the button for the elevator, her mind focused on her car in the parking lot. Home. She needed to go home. This whole night had been a bad idea.

She only made it to her car, parked at the back of the quiet lot, before the pain refused to be held back any longer. The sob she'd held back all these years broke free, and she sagged against the driver's side door of her Jag as the tears washed down her cheeks.

How long she stood there sobbing, she didn't know, but footsteps sounded on the pavement somewhere beyond her, echoing around the quiet lot. She sniffled, clutched her keys tightly in her hand, ready to fend off an attacker if need be, and turned her head. Tyler jogged in her direction, the backdrop of the street lights illuminating him from behind. Like a goddamn angel from Heaven. He came to a stop in front of her, his tall, broad form towering over her, his chest heaving.

His warm breaths misted in the cool night air, and one corner of his mouth curled upward. "You're not making this easy, babe."

His voice was still hauntingly familiar. She reached out a tentative hand, needing to touch him, to know she hadn't imagined him.

Tyler flinched, jerking away from her, his eyes wild and

searching, body tensing. He drew a slow, deep breath, blew it out, and squared his shoulders, but he didn't relax. Nor did he pull any farther away.

Cassie reached out again, searching the face she'd know in the dark. Prominent cheekbones. A strong jaw. He'd lost weight. The planes and angles of his face had become more pronounced, his skin paler, eyes sunken and rimmed in shadow. He had a haunted look about him now. "Tell me I'm not dreaming, Ty."

"I'll do you one better." He cupped her face in the warmth of his palms and stared for moment before he leaned down and captured her lips. His mouth was warm and familiar, but it wasn't the passionate kiss she remembered. He kissed her softly at first, before settling his mouth more firmly over hers. His fingers trembled as they stroked her face.

Lost in the moment, in the fantasy, she leaned into him. Any minute now she'd wake up, and he'd go *poof*, and she'd find herself alone in bed. Right then, though, it was the best damn kiss she'd had in a long time, and God help her, she lifted onto her toes to get more of him. If she was dreaming, she had every intention of milking it.

When she laid her palms against his chest, needing his warmth, to feel the solidity of his body, he flinched again and jerked back. Confusion flicked over his features before recognition settled in his gaze. He fisted his hands in her hair, pulling her back to him, and rested his forehead against hers. "Jesus, I missed you."

His words jarred through her, and her hope sank into her toes again. Tyler wouldn't have said that to her. The last time she'd seen him, they'd fought. She'd said horrible things to him that day. He'd proposed to her, down on one knee and looking gorgeous in his uniform, and she'd turned him down flat. She'd lied. Had looked him right in the eye and told him she didn't love him, that he was a fling.

She'd lied through her teeth, because she couldn't do it. He was deploying, and she couldn't be that wife who waited every day wondering if he'd come home alive. She couldn't lose another person she loved. She'd lost her brother in Iraq five years ago…after losing their mother five years before that. Their family hadn't been the same since Nick's death. Her *baba* had shut her out, lost to his grief. She couldn't, wouldn't, go through that again, lose one more person.

Except the joke had been on her. She'd waited anyway, had worried anyway, and when Tyler hadn't come home, the bottom had dropped out of her world. His death had left her struggling. To move on. To release the guilt caught in her chest. To live.

All of which only brought a multitude of questions and pain. Three years had passed. They were different. *She* was different. His death had changed her. His experiences out there had certainly changed him. She'd heard from so many of her clients whose sons and daughters had come home from the war, forever changed. Who knew what he'd gone through over there?

So why the hell would he miss *her*? Why would he even want her after the way she'd treated him? *She* wouldn't.

Drawing strength from the pain threatening to swallow her, she braced her hands against his chest and shoved him away from her. He stumbled back a step, brow furrowing in confusion. Keys clutched in her hand, she pointed the fob in his direction and glared at him. "I don't know what the hell kind of game you're playing, Ty, but you made your point, okay? This isn't funny anymore."

He opened his mouth, but she hit the key fob and climbed inside her car, slamming the door. She hit the button to start the engine, dropped the shifter into drive, and stomped on the gas pedal. She didn't breathe or blink or even dare to look back until he'd become little more than a fading speck behind her.

Acknowledgments

No book gets written without a lot of support, and I have to take a moment to thank a few people. First, I have to thank my editor, Jessie, for seeing the story within the story, and helping shape this book into something that wowed me at the end.

Also to my critique partners, Sharon Struth and Skye Jones, for their friendship and support. I'd go crazy without you guys.

And I can't forget my agent, Dawn Dowdle, for everything that makes her who she is.

About the Author

JM Stewart is a coffee and chocolate addict who lives in the Pacific Northwest with her husband, two sons, and two very spoiled dogs. She's a hopeless romantic who believes everybody should have their happily ever after and has been devouring romance novels for as long as she can remember. Writing them has become her obsession.

Learn more at:

AuthorJMStewart.com

Facebook.com/AuthorJMStewart

Twitter: @JMStewartWriter

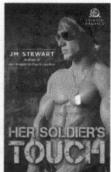